The Fastest Draw

ALSO BY MAX BRAND

The Fastest Draw

MAX BRAND

DODD, MEAD & COMPANY

New York

The Fastest Draw was first published in four parts in *Argosy Magazine* in 1925 under the title *Señor Jingle Bells*, written under the pseudonym of David Manning, and subsequently in book form by Chelsea House in 1927.

Published by Dodd, Mead & Company, Inc.
71 Fifth Avenue, New York, N.Y. 10003
Manufactured in the United States of America
First Edition

1   2   3   4   5   6   7   8   9   10

Library of Congress Cataloging-in-Publication Data

Brand, Max, 1892–1944.
    The fastest draw.

    (Silver star westerns)
    I. Title.   II. Series: Silver star western.
PS3511.A87F37   1987   813'.52   87-19970
ISBN 0-396-09078-8

The Fastest Draw

1

Gloryville held its breath, and out of the blue mountains in the east and the brown mountains in the west peace rolled over the little town. It was a peace so very deep that through the stillness one could hear the waters of Glory Creek gurgling around the concrete pillars which upheld the bridge, or the splash of a fish in the shallows where the willows made a shade.

However, this was neither a dull nor an unprofitable time in Gloryville; for men were waiting for a show, and it was that thrilling moment after the audience is seated and before the orchestra begins. Gloryville took note of itself, numbered heads, regarded faces, considered the weather and other details, and settled itself as comfortably as possible, for there was no impatience.

It did not matter, really, how long the performance was delayed, since when it came it was sure to be worth while.

Then, accompanied by a stir at the door of the hotel, one of the chief performers came upon the stage.

That was Jim Sladen, with the flat face of an old Indian, and a thick, wrinkled neck, and long, gorilla arms. He wore two guns, and could use them both. That, it might be said, was the cue to the piece—he was sure to use them to-day! He stood for a time to let every one see him and to see every one in his turn. Then he asked

1

for a chair, and although he would have had to serve himself on another day, a chair was now instantly surrendered to him.

He thanked the donor with a grunt and canted himself back in the chair, after settling his guns so that the holsters hung free and easy at his sides.

A low, brief, ominous murmur greeted Mr. Sladen. Men spoke to one another out of the corners of their mouths without removing their eyes from Jim. It might have seemed that they were eager for his fall, since there was something akin to hatred in their eyes.

But as a matter of fact, Jim Sladen was popular in Gloryville. He had lived there for the last twenty years of his life. His fame was built around the place, and his fame was large. More people in the world knew Jim Sladen of Gloryville by name than had ever looked upon the town itself; particularly since he disposed of the Oklahoma killer "Kid" Lorraine three years before.

Therefore, Jim Sladen was known and popular, but all of his popularity could not save him from these hungry eyes which searched him through and through and decided that he was a gladiator fit to be served up for their delectation upon this stage. No, they did not hate Jim Sladen, but they were very willing that he should be killed, publicly, for their amusement. Here another murmur grew and attention swung to the second-story balcony of Señor Alvarez's house just across the street from the hotel, for in that balcony sat a second actor in the piece.

This was the daughter of Alvarez, called by the pleasantly alliterative name of Alicia—a softly musical title of which she was well worthy. For she was a dusky beauty, with perhaps a double share of Indian blood showing in her smoky eyes, but with delicately made features and the grace of a bird in the movements of her head and hands.

2

She was just sixteen, although she appeared to Anglo-Saxon eyes a vital bit older; now all the bloom of young womanhood was in her cheeks and in her eyes, and sometimes when she smiled at her mother, she was only a little child. This, however, was not often.

Considered as a whole, she was dressed to fit her part. She had a jeweled comb in her softly rolled black hair, misted over by the filmy lace of a delicate mantilla; and the gown she wore had been finished in the small hours of the morning by her mother, so that Alicia might be fit to have the gaze of the town rest upon her. This was to be expected, if she showed herself; and Señor Alvarez saw no reason why he should not display the most attractive portion of his possessions on such an occasion, no matter what Anglo-Saxon taste might choose. Particularly since Alicia was really the headwater and the spring out of which the ensuing drama was to arise.

For Alicia had been looked upon by Jim Sladen and coveted by him; and Jim Sladen's interest in the ore mine being equally looked upon and coveted by Señor Alvarez, they came to a quick agreement without, however, consulting Alicia. She submitted with some grace, under the admonishing eye of her mother, but having wept for a few minutes on the neck of that mother, she shrugged her shoulders and looked about her for some amusement before the marriage rites should be performed.

There were a hundred youths near Gloryville or in it who would have been glad to let Alicia amuse herself to her heart's content with them. Unfortunately, she picked out not a boy, but a man—and that man was none other than Frank Yarnell, bound for Montana and stopping in Gloryville only overnight. He was the dry stubble into which Alicia happened to drop her match, and the flame she raised glared in the eyes of all Gloryville.

He had to ride on toward Montana the very next day

when Jim Sladen, receiving the news from mischievous gossips, rushed down from the mine bent on destruction. He found Yarnell gone, and such was his passion that he flung his horse blindly to the north for two days of useless riding in the vain hope of coming upon the trail of Yarnell.

After that he returned to Gloryville and hunted up Señor Alvarez. The Mexican assured him that it is as difficult to keep a girl of sixteen from flirting as it is to keep a bird off the wing. Each loves a natural element.

He saw Alicia herself, who told him that he was breaking her heart and reduced him to perspiration and confusion in less than a minute. After this he retreated to the veranda of the hotel, which was a rostrum from which many and important statements had been issued, but none more exciting than this of Jim Sladen's. For he declared that he would destroy Frank Yarnell root and branch, and that he never would rest, once he discovered the hiding place of the latter. Sladen had made such statements before, and had executed them without any particular noise of trumpets; but this was different, and the difference lay in Frank Yarnell.

For Yarnell was a natural savage. He was one of those long men with big bones who look twenty pounds less than their actual weight. He had hands like an ape, with huge joints and blunt finger tips, and hair growing like fur over the back of the hand. He loved battle as other men love food when they are starved or liquor when they are thirsty.

He looked upon one who did battle with him with a sort of affection and gratitude. He had been known to smile almost fondly upon those who insulted him, so greatly did he rejoice in the opportunity to destroy!

It mattered not with what weapons he was to work. He was ever with a knife in his hand; he was of the medieval school in the intricacy of his knife work; but

4

best of all he enjoyed those delicious moments when his hands closed upon the bare flesh of his enemy.

And although men admired his prowess, they thought of Yarnell with a little touch of horror; there was a ghastly story of what he had done to a professional wrestler in an Arizona barroom, eight years before, and there were other tales less widely known but almost equally inhuman.

Such was the man whom Sladen had announced that he would destroy, and therefore it was that the public held its breath with the joy of suspense. And after a little while a furious message came to town from Yarnell himself. He had not gone into hiding from Jim Sladen or from any other man.

He had merely ridden to the north because his business carried him there, but he was going to make it his special affair now to return directly to Gloryville, find Alicia Alvarez, and marry her. And if Jim Sladen didn't like that idea, he announced to the public that he would dissect Mr. Sladen, and, selecting his liver, which he assured the people would be found to be yellow, he would feed that liver to the dogs.

It was a letter directed to the hotel keeper, and there was a postscript requesting that the said letter be tacked up against the wall in the lobby.

It was done, of course. And men rode in fifty miles to look at that famous and terrible challenge. As for Jim Sladen, he fell into such a paroxysm of rage when he heard about the thing that he went down to the hotel and shot over the four corners of the letter, which increased the excitement of the public and served as a sort of answer to the letter itself.

All these things had happened some time before, but not long enough ago to dull the edge of interest, and the letter was still hanging on the wall of the hotel lobby when another letter came from Frank Yarnell, stating plainly that he would return to Gloryville upon this Thursday morning. He hoped everyone but the sheriff would be there, and that he particularly would be delighted to see Mr. James Sladen, whether on foot or on horseback, with rifle, revolver, or knife—or, best of all, with bared hands. With any or all of these weapons he announced that he would kill Mr. Sladen before Thursday noon and that he would marry Alicia before Thursday night.

"What'll you do when he comes to your house?" people asked Alvarez.

He would shrug his shoulders and roll up his eyes.

"What *can* one do with such a man, señor?"

After all, he was right, in the opinion of the sober-minded. Why should a whole family stand in danger of being blotted out because a girl does not wish to marry a certain man? Indeed, it was not even certain that Alicia would refuse the terrible Yarnell.

There was something in her dark, languorous eyes which made men shiver a little as they looked up to her on that low balcony, moving her fan slowly to show its rich filigree, the slenderness of her wrist, the delicacy of her hand. She was for all the world like something put up for sale. The special horror now was that the price in which she was interested seemed to be blood.

Two of the principals in the drama having been brought upon the same stage, there now remained the long delay before the third member of the cast came into view. It was for him that Gloryville held its breath, and a little moan of excitement ran up and down the street when a whisper announced that a cloud of dust, as if raised by a horseman, had been seen along the eastern trail, coming down the side of Glory Mountain.

It was the direction from which Frank Yarnell was expected, and, in preparation for the last great moment,

6

all men moved away from the immediate vicinity of Jim Sladen.

He was left deserted upon the veranda of the hotel which might soon be swept with bullets.

2

That eastern trail now dipped along the mountainside in full view of the entire length of the street of Gloryville. It was still no better than a bridle path, but the reckless mule skinners had forced their teams up that wretched excuse for a road until it was deep with churned dust. So the white cloud arose high above the rider until, when he was not far from the edge of the town, he paused and the wind lifted the mist away from him.

He was still at such a distance that they could not make him out clearly, but he was seen to dismount and to be busy about his horse and about himself. It was Yarnell, certainly, calmly preparing himself before he entered the town and the lists of battle!

Now the horseman mounted again and proceeded at a walk down the last of the slope and into the level of the town. He disappeared in a first winding of the street; then he came suddenly into view of the hotel and its crowded vicinity.

But as he did so there was a muttering of disappointment. For it was not Frank Yarnell at all, but presumably some Mexican caballero, flashing with metal trappings like a knight in armor. Great silver conchos lined his narrow trousers; golden fretwork weighted down his sombrero; with solid silver his saddle was inlaid; as he went he carried his own music with him—several little bells sounding pleasantly on the bridle of his horse.

Sladen himself gave him a name: "It ain't Yarnell. It's a jingle bells!"

Jingle Bells proceeded slowly into the wider space in front of the hotel, where he paused and looked about him with much deliberation. There was little doubt about his nationality now. His hair was polished jet; his hands and his face were the deepest brown; and his pause outside the town had been, with typical Mexican vanity, simply to furbish himself and his ornaments until they shone again. He came as freshly into Gloryville on that hot day as a débutante into a ballroom.

Indeed, there was something markedly feminine about the stranger. Gloryville muttered like a distant waterfall as it regarded him, for although your Westerner is not altogether blind to some fashions in beauty, beauty in a man he does not appreciate.

And the youth in silver and gold with the crimson silken sash around his waist was more than handsome. His eyes were as big and as soft as the eyes of a girl; his chin and his cheeks were modeled with the indescribable delicacy of a woman's, and even in spite of his gloves it could be seen that his hands were long and slender. He dropped one of those hands upon his hip and looked about him with much effrontery, which did not serve to lessen the impression in his disfavor.

When he spoke, moreover, his voice was very soft and gentle, of a truly feminine quality, and caused the stalwart gentry of Gloryville to grunt. They were so annoyed by the whole appearance of this fellow that they almost forgot the impending coming of Frank Yarnell.

8

"Is this a show?" asked Jingle Bells; and his red bay horse, hardly less dainty and beautiful than its rider, tossed its head and made the bells chime with a little shower of golden music. "Is this a show or a funeral, or what?"

No one chose to answer him. He continued his survey until his glance rested upon the fair Alicia on the balcony above him, and with a dexterous touch of his knees he swayed his stallion closer to that lovely girl. His sombrero he raised and exposed his black hair, combed slick and glistening upon his head.

He said in Spanish almost too perfect to be Mexican: "Señorita, they are all too sad to speak to me, but you will tell a stranger. There is a speaking thing in your eyes, lady!"

This he said not softly, but with a brazen impudence which actually made him raise his voice, and in this fashion half of the people who were gathered there heard and understood him. A little chuckle of savage anticipation passed around the waiting audience while they turned their gaze upon the formidable bulk of Jim Sladen, now lolling deep in his chair on the veranda.

As for Alicia, she too turned her glance toward that lionlike figure and then bit her lip as she glanced back at the stranger. It was all very well to have a pair of gringos fight for her sake, but when it came to offering up as a sacrifice this exquisite young gentleman, her heart changed and swelled in her.

And when she looked down into his big, brown, gentle eyes Alicia swayed forward a little and grew a trifle dizzy.

She managed to murmur: "Beware!"

"A thousand thanks!" said the youth, his voice even more distinctly audible than before. "But beware of what?"

He turned in the saddle and swept the scene with another deliberate glance.

9

"Is there a dog here?" His stare fastened upon Jim Sladen. "Ah," said he, "I see that there is—and a bulldog, at that!"

All of this was still in Spanish, regardless of the fact that every one in that Southwestern town understood Spanish as well as they understood English, or a little bit better. Regardless, too, of the rising of Jim Sladen from his chair at the edge of the veranda.

"Señorita," said this impertinent youngster, who had surely not completed his two-and-twentieth year, "I kiss your hand. Adios!"

He waved his hat to her; he bestowed upon her a languishing smile, which caused the heart of poor Alicia to leap into the hollow of her throat, and brought a groan of disapproval from the other bystanders, while Señora Alvarez spoke sharply in an undertone to her daughter.

"What do I care?" said Alicia almost savagely. "Let them see if they wish. He is so beautiful and so wonderful! Did you see his eyes, mother? And now he is riding to Señor Sladen!"

The young stranger, in fact, had crossed the street among the angry murmurs of the spectators, and now he made straight for the terrible hero Sladen who stood swelling with rage.

"Young feller," boomed Sladen, staggered by the reckless impertinence of the youth, "what d'you aim to be after?"

"I was told by the beautiful girl across the street," said Jingle Bells, "that I was in danger. I have come to you to find out what it may be. Can you tell me, señor?"

"Look here," said Jim Sladen, gathering his wrath, but saving it as a precious thing which must not be hastily expended—"look here, young feller, can you speak English?"

10

"When I see such a face," said the youth, turning in the saddle and lifting his sombrero, as if to honor Alicia with every mention of her name, "when I see such a face, señor, it is with difficulty that I can speak English—or even think in it. However, I may be able to manage a few words."

Jim Sladen licked his wide lips and rolled his flat eyes up and down the graceful figure of the horseman, as though selecting in what places he would strike him with death, or in what place his thick, strong fingers would fasten to pluck the dainty fellow from his seat.

"Jingle Bells," said Jim Sladen, letting his words writhe out of sardonic lips, "I dunno who you are, and I dunno that I give a damn. But d'you know me?"

The insult slipped from the smiling face of the boy like water from the proverbial feathers.

"I do not know you, señor," he said, "but I guess from your manner of talking that you are a great man."

A growl formed in Sladen's throat.

"I'm Jim Sladen," he said. "Might it be that you've ever heard of me?"

The other squinted in thought.

"Sladen?" he said. "Sladen? Ah, yes, señor—you are that celebrated murderer, are you not?"

Suppose that a child should step up to a lion and, smiling, strike it in the face between the eyes, upon the wrinkled forehead. Suppose that lightning should glimmer in a stormy sky and that a fool, with laughter, should step into its flaming pathway.

Suppose anything wonderful and reckless, and yet it would be hard to imagine the shock which the assembled citizens of Gloryville felt as they heard this speech. It stiffened men in their chairs. It caused expectant grins to freeze into gaping mouths of horror.

It caused smiling women to clasp their hands sud-

11

denly, expecting the death stroke to fall. As for Jim Sladen, it made him recoil a pace with a heavy heel.

"Now," said he, "it ain't possible that I'm hearin' you right!"

"Why," said the cavalier, "perhaps I am wrong. Perhaps you are not the man who hunted Dick Jeffreys until you found him sitting in his cabin and then shot him through the back, señor?"

Sladen opened his dull eyes.

"And you are not," continued the silken voice of Jingle Bells, "the man who murdered young Tim Houlahan when you found him with a wound in his right arm. You are not that Jim Sladen. You are another, but with a face as ugly as his own!"

This speech he delivered in English and with such an accent that all who heard him realized that, in spite of brown skin and black hair, this was Anglo-Saxon blood; and that this was not Latin impudence but true American recklessness. And having spoken, moreover, he sat his saddle, looking down at Jim Sladen with a purely Yankee grin. There was no mistaking him.

Jim Sladen recovered from his amazement sufficiently to see that he must kill his man and kill at once.

"You cantankerous young rat!" he shouted. "You yaller-skinned—"

His words were cut across by the slash of the stranger's quirt which seamed the face of Sladen with white from ear to mouth and brought a scream of fury and pain from his lips, while he clutched at his gun.

But Jingle Bells did not wait for the explosion of the gun. He followed his whipstroke by coming out of his saddle like a hawk sliding out of the sky at a rabbit beneath. Like the stoop of the hawk, inescapable and swift, he struck Jim Sladen.

One hand caught the wrist of the gunfighter and twisted it with a grip that burned the flesh against the bones

12

until the gun rattled on the veranda floor; one arm caught the bull neck of the warrior in its elbow crook and crushed the air out. Then the numbed wrist of Jim Sladen was relaxed, and a knife point tickled his ribs lightly.

Jingle Bells stepped back from his victim, balancing the long, heavy knife flat in the palm of his hand—a Mexican trick of handling that grisly weapon before it is flung like a streak of light that goes out in flesh and blood. And Jim Sladen, fumbling at his crushed throat with his right hand, and gripping the butt of his second revolver with the other, weighed his chances and decided that the knife could beat the gun.

He gave one wild glance to the horrified, bewildered faces which he saw everywhcre around him. Then he turned and stumbled blindly for the door of the hotel.

"Stop!" commanded Jingle Bells.

Jim Sladen stopped with a shudder and wheeled around.

"You have forgotten one half of your courage!" sneered Jingle Bells, and kicked the fallen revolver toward its owner.

But Sladen paid no heed to that. He turned again and strode on through the door of the hotel with a moan of shame and rage.

Behind him, Jingle Bells was dusting himself with fastidious care.

"Why, what a dirty beast that Sladen is!" he said. "As dusty as the road my horse steps on!"

3

After this, fumbling in a breast pocket, he produced a sack of tobacco, but fumbled in vain for papers. They were offered to him by a bull-throated waddy from the Yerxa outfit.

"Partner," said he, "what might your name be?"

The stranger made a cigarette with a flash of his sun-browned fingers, lighted a match with a snapping thumb nail, and breathed smoke in and out before he answered, but all the while he seemed to be considering his reply.

"I've picked up enough names to do for two or three," he said, showing his fine, white teeth, as he smiled. "The last place I drifted through, they called me Miss Mañana. But I guess Sladen has given me a working name for Gloryville. 'Jingle Bells' will do for me—or 'Jingle' is good enough. I keep the fancy names for my horse.

"My horse, however," said the gay youth, "has a name which he is very proud of. I assure you that although I allow the greatest familiarities to be taken with me and that I have not the slightest objection to such a title as Jingle, I should be very much hurt if any one were to fail to give my horse his full name, which is Monsieur le Duc!"

He turned sharply upon the beautiful blood-bay stallion which, at the sound of its name or at the turning of its master, receded a pace with a forefoot and bowed like a circus horse on parade.

"Look!" said a girl who was passing down the street with her father. "Look at that wonderful animal. Can we stop and watch it a moment?"

"The trouble may not be over," said her companion.

14

"I understand this fellow Sladen has been put out of the way—some accident must have happened to him. But there is still apt to be trouble in the air with such a crowd gathered. We'd better go on, Peggy."

He uttered this in the full tone of a man accustomed to authority, and loosened the reins of his horse to pass on. Jingle, who had turned toward his horse at the same time, heard the remark and, what was more, saw the girl with him.

The Señorita Alicia sat just opposite in her balcony, wearing her most intriguing smile, which could have drawn a glance from a saint as surely as a magnet can pick up a grain of iron dust, but Jingle saw her no more than if she had been obscured by the densest of clouds. She was no doubt the more beautiful in feature, but there is a loveliness of spirit which shines through some women, young or old; they carry with them a still-burning lamp which age and sorrow cannot dim.

Such a radiance shone in the face of the girl on horseback. Some in their haste failed to see it, but the eyes of Jingle noted all things, and at a glance.

He had his gold-trimmed sombrero off in an instant, and the sun glittered on his sleek black hair as he bowed to the strangers.

"I give you my word, sir," said he, "that all danger has passed. Gloryville is as quiet now as Sunday and, as you suggest, a fortunate accident has removed Mr. Sladen."

At this there was a grim, half-subdued chuckle from the bystanders, repressed because the awe of the thing which had just been witnessed had not yet passed away. Having seen the tiger's claw, they were not yet able to appreciate to the full the velvet qualities of this youth.

The elderly gentleman on horseback, although he did not appreciate the cause of the chuckle, smiled; and his smile was directed to the flaming gaudiness of the young man's attire, particularly to the flaring sash of crimson silk which girdled his waist.

"If that is the case," he remarked, "I suppose we may stay for a moment."

The youth turned to that same bull-necked puncher who had loaned him the cigarette papers.

"Introduce me," said he, "to this gentleman."

The cowpuncher was glad enough to step to the center of the stage even in such a minor rôle.

"Mr. Swain and Miss Swain," said he, "I got the pleasure of havin' you meet, Mr.—er—Mr.—"

"Jingle," said the youth carelessly.

"Mr. Jingle," said the puncher, turning very red.

The two on horseback acknowledged the introduction with broad smiles; for, not having witnessed the last scene, they could not help taking him for a joke and a very good one. However, he endured their smiles without the slightest embarrassment and jumped down from the veranda of the hotel to shake hands.

The middle-aged rancher, when he felt the touch of that soft palm, grunted his disapproval; as for the girl, she could not control the shadow of scorn which drifted across her brow.

But she managed to say: "I think I've never seen such a beautiful horse, Mr. Jingle. He has plenty of speed, I should say!"

"He is the wind," said Jingle, without modesty.

"And blood, eh?" asked Mr. Swain.

"Upon one side," said Jingle seriously, "he traces his ancestry to the most illustrious families. The royalty of three great nations, sir, has been intimate with his fathers."

Both Mr. Swain, and his daughter looked to each other, and smiled wisely.

"His ancestors really," said Jingle in continuation, "have been much written about. Even the details of their pri-

16

vate lives have appeared in many publications, and the births and the marriages have been announced in headlines in the journals. Their public appearances were always the cause of great demonstrations. But even in the bluest of blood there is sometimes a shadow of a stain. As for the mother of Monsieur le Duc—"

"Is that his name?" laughed the girl. "Monsieur le Duc?"

He bowed to her.

"I thank you," said he, "for that French 'u.' And so does Monsieur le Duc, I am sure."

At this, he turned to the stallion, and the glorious creature made its step back, as before, and bowed its head until the tips of its mane touched the dust. Miss Margaret Swain laughed with a soft little caress in her voice and her eyes, as she watched this performance, and saw the horse after rising, so far forget its dignity as to step closer, and rest its muzzle upon the shoulder of its master.

"You were telling us about the faint shadow on the blood of Monsieur le Duc," she suggested. "Or was it the French 'u' in which you were interested?"

"In both," said he, and his answering smile was again that broad, Yankee grin which the people of Gloryville had noted before. "But concerning his parentage—his father, as I have said, was of that ancient and noble family of which I have been telling you. His mother was a person of beauty, and distinction of manner. She could not go abroad without being surrounded by admiration. And yet—I regret with all my heart that I must say it —her family was really nothing. If I were to put her father beside Monsieur le Duc, he would blush for shame, I assure you. In fact, across his coat of arms lies a bar sinister. It was a mesalliance!"

Miss Swain broke into the heartiest laughter. At which, the Señorita Alicia across the way puckered her brow in a black frown, until she remembered that frowns are not good for the smoothness of the forehead.

Here a stern voice broke in from a rider who had progressed up the street unnoticed in the general interest which was taken in the scene around the stallion.

"Gents," called out this new arrival, "I'm lookin' for Jim Sladen. Where might he have gone? Where's Jim Sladen!"

This directed all attention upon him, and they saw none other than terrible Frank Yarnell dismounting before the hotel and striding toward them. The murmur of his dreaded name passed round and round the circle. The rancher, hearing it, picked up his daughter with a glance, and they rode off together down the street.

"Here you, 'Ribbons!' " said Frank Yarnell bluntly to Jingle. "If you been here long enough showin' yourself, maybe you know where Jim Sladen is? Hell and fire, gents, are you all gone dumb? Ain't none of you ever heard of that skunk Sladen?"

He was greeted by an embarrassed silence. In a way, it might be said that Jim Sladen was the champion of the town. Not that he in any way represented it, but at least he lived in it, and such a residence gave it a claim upon him, and gave him a claim upon it.

The hardy cowpunchers who had come to see Jim Sladen do battle with the stranger looked at one another, and blushed with patriotic shame. For who could tell Yarnell that the other man of might had been brushed from his path by this dapper youth? Certainly no one could have such matchless effrontery!

So a silence fell upon the street, and left Frank Yarnell staring about him in a growing fury, as if convinced that a practical joke was being played upon him.

He was a mighty man, this Frank Yarnell, dish-faced, with a long, protruding, rocklike jaw; and now that his temper was up he might have stood for his picture as

one of hell's ugliest devils. In such a mood, he could not
help but look about him for a victim.

He had come prepared to kill or be killed, and to have
the victim removed maddened him. Now he strode a
long pace nearer to Jingle.

"Hey, Ribbons!" he said to the youth.

"You have done me a very bad turn," Jingle explained
gently. "You have interrupted me in the midst of a pleasant conversation. I might almost say, my friend, that you
drove the lady and the gentleman away!"

Yarnell glared at him until, taking into account that
this was a mere fop of the range, or hardly of the cow
country at all, to judge by his language, he decided to
master the more violent show of his rage, and inflict
upon the younger man some minor humiliation.

"What," said he, "might you be?"

"I'm a traveler," Jingle replied.

"Travelin' toward what?" asked Yarnell.

"Amusement," answered Jingle, still with his pleasant
smile.

"Son," said Yarnell, rubbing the hairy back of his hand
against his chin, "I dunno that you ain't a queer one!
What's your name?"

"Jingle."

"I ain't askin' about your hoss—"

"My horse?" exclaimed Jingle. "By no means! The
name of my horse, Mr. Yarnell, is Monsieur le Duc."

"Monsoor what?" snapped Yarnell.

"Le Duc."

"Le Dick? What kind of a name is that?"

"The French 'u,' " said Jingle, smiling upon the other
with a singular lack of mirth. "Monsieur le Duc is his
name."

He turned to the horse.

"Monsieur le Duc," said he, "this is the famous Frank
Yarnell."

Monsieur le Duc bowed in his usual manner, but Yarnell merely scowled.

"You know me do you? Then you know what I'm here for."

"For Mr. Sladen? I am so sorry to tell you that somone else called before you."

"What?"

"Besides, Mr. Yarnell, you have not noticed that Monsieur le Duc has bowed to you?"

"I don't want to hear no funny talk," said Yarnell sourly. "I ain't a funny man. I hate a joke. I want to know what you mean when you say that somebody else called upon Sladen before me?"

"I thought that I spoke clearly. I said, sir, that another person called upon Mr. Sladen before you came."

"You mean Sladen busted loose, and shot up somebody, and had to climb out of town?"

"The reverse, sir."

"Hey?"

"Mr. Sladen fell into an argument. In the midst of it, he slipped, and fell so badly that his pride, I'm afraid, is broken to bits forever. In the meantime, I am sorry to remind you that my horse has bowed to you, sir."

"Young feller," said Yarnell, who had been on the verge of turning away from this unprofitable conversation, "I dunno what you're drivin' at. Only I tell you that I ain't a gent that likes jokes. What you can do for me is to tell me the name of the gent that beat up Sladen."

"Poor Mr. Sladen had his argument with me."

Yarnell turned back with an oath, and dropped both of his hands upon his hips, and expressed himself feelingly.

"I've seen nacheral born liars, and gents with enough brass in 'em to furnish a factory for cartridges for a year; but blast my heart if I ever met up with the likes of you!"

"You are explicit," said Jingle, smiling again, and letting his soft brown eyes dwell upon the face of the other. "In the meantime there is the horse—"

"What d'you mean that I should do to the hoss, boy?"

"What he has done to you," said young Mr. Jingle. "Bow to him, Mr. Yarnell!"

Such great facts, coming by surprise, must dawn upon the mind slowly. It took Yarnell longer than Sladen had required, for the very good reason that Yarnell considered himself a far better man than Sladen, and because, perhaps, he was. He favored the youngster with a brief smile, and then jerked his head toward the watering trough.

"Some gents get drunk on booze, and some on fresh air, and some get pretty sloppy just over their clothes," observed Frank Yarnell. "Young feller, I aim to tame you down considerable before I'm through with you. And cool you down, too. Over yonder is a trough all full of water, and this here is a mighty hot day. Might be you'd like to go take a dip over yonder?"

And he looked around him over the circle of the surrounding faces. To his astonishment, he found not a trace of a smile. All was only the most intent, the most solemn interest.

From behind him, and from behind the youth in the brilliant sash, people were crowding back. It was very much as if they expected bullets might be flying before long.

The purring voice of Jingle was saying again: "I live on intimate terms with his grace. I may even pride myself in saying that he reposes every confidence in me. What will he think, sir, if I allow him to be insulted in this public fashion? He will certainly go about getting himself another master."

"It ain't a joke then?" said Frank Yarnell, partly to himself. "I'm to bow to that hoss?"

"Of course!"

21

"Jingle—if that's your name—doggone me if I don't hate to do it. I'm a nacherally peace-lovin' man."

He began to sway himself a little from side to side, as though he needed some artificial stimulus to awaken his full ferocity.

"But they's something that tells me, Mr. Jingle, that you're plumb tired of inhabitin' hereabouts. If you aim to get out of my way, you better start runnin' because what I chase a gent with goes pretty fast. It don't dodge none. It most usually don't have to."

"Besides," continued Jingle, as if he had not been interrupted, "you have not only failed to bow to Monsieur, you have also mispronounced his name. It is a point upon which he is very sensitive. I have seen him fly into a rage because I have permitted such a thing. Mr. Yarnell," he added with a slight change in voice, "I am waiting!"

"You're waitin' for what? For me?" thundered Yarnell. "Why, I'll get you ready for plantin', you young sap! I'll—"

He found vigorous words had failed him, and reached for his gun to make it talk for him.

It was to be observed that at either hip of Mr. Jingle hung a holster not of any common or garden variety, but of the finest black morocco, varnished so that it shone like a mold of black glass when the sun struck fairly upon it. The outer rims of these holsters were decorated with a filigree of heavy gold, beautiful and fantastic work such as Mexican artificers are capable of producing.

And in the upper center of each holster there was a clasp set off with rich red jewels—rubies, perhaps, although they appeared too large to be such precious stones. The flaps which covered the butts of his guns, however, were opened and tucked inside the cases, and for a very manifest reason—which was that the handles of those weapons were of the finest pearl, white and glistening as the snow which lodges above timber line all the year.

One could hardly imagine that such guns were for use; and no such thought passed through the brain of Mr. Yarnell, yet his motion toward his own weapon was as fast as light by force of habit.

It was as fast as light, but that of Jingle was still faster. His slender fingers flicked back; the pearl handles twitched brilliantly into the light of the sun with a long length of blue steel following, and the gun at the left hip of Jingle exploded just as the fingers of Yarnell clasped the butt of his own trusty revolver.

The bullet struck Yarnell's holster, jerked his belt around and the gun out of his hand, and left the man-killer helpless in front of a pair of steady weapons which looked him over and up and down out of their black eyes—looked him over hungrily, dwelling on his heart and on his head.

"Monsieur le Duc," said Jingle, "is waiting."

Yarnell moistened his white lips.

"Monsieur le Duc," Jingle repeated, "is waiting patiently."

"What," asked Yarnell, "in the name o' heaven, d'you you want me to do?"

"A bow," said Jingle. "A low, beautiful bow to the gentleman."

The eyes of Yarnell flashed around the circle. One, two, three—he counted the smiles; the others were still stunned and gaping at what they had seen.

"I'll see you damned first!" gasped the gunfighter. "Before I'll—"

The right-hand gun exploded; the sombrero of Yarnell arose from his head, twisting around and around, and sailed sedately toward the watering trough, upon the surface of which it settled.

"It's murder!" breathed Yarnell. "Gents, are you gonna stand by and see—"

"Monsieur le Duc," said Jingle softly through his teeth,

"is unaccustomed to waiting. A low bow, Mr. Yarnell, or—"

The left-hand gun steadied at the very heart of Yarnell, and that gentleman discovered suddenly that there were unsuspected hinges in the small of his back.

He bowed!

"And now," said Jingle, "his name. Monsieur le Duc for his part has been very pleased to speak the name of Mr. Yarnell. Did I hear you speak, Monsieur?"

At that, the stallion tossed his head and whinnied softly.

"You recognize the name, no doubt," said Jingle.

"I do," whispered Yarnell through his teeth.

"Then—"

"Monsoor le Dook," said Yarnell, "I'm pleased to know you."

"Duc!" corrected Jingle. "Monsieur le Duc!"

"Damnation!" groaned Yarnell. "Monsieur le Duc!"

"Ah," said Jingle, "I see you have a talent for languages!"

4

When fat Sheriff Walter Long came back from the mountains that evening, he went to "Hen" Pearson, who ran the hotel and also distributed news. Hen Pearson had a mind arranged like a newspaper file, both for the variety of his mental contents and for the orderliness with which he could bring them forth.

"You been missed," said Hen Pearson. "Folks has been

expectin' you around these parts to keep them two bloody mankillers apart."

The sheriff settled himself into a chair facing the host. Each of them overflowed the seat and bulked soft and thick over the arms. They smiled upon each other. There is nothing so mutually approving as a pair of fat men, nothing so sympathetic.

"Why should I stand around to take tickets?" said the sheriff, when he had so massaged a cigar with his moist fingers that it was properly constituted for drawing well. "Why should I hang around," he went on, "when there was a couple of gents ready to do my work for me?"

"A couple of gents like which?"

"Like Yarnell and Sladen. If they ain't cut out, both of them, to stretch rope, why damn my eyes if I ain't willing to eat my hat! I figgered on stayin' away and lettin' the party finish up all quiet by itself. Well, where are the corpses?"

"If you was to go straight east, you'd find Sladen somewhere on the mountain. If you was to go straight west, you'd find Yarnell headin' in the opposite direction, and leggin' it fast."

The sheriff groaned his disappointment.

"They lost their nerve when they seen each other, eh? I figgered maybe that would be it."

"You got a fine imagination," said Hen Pearson dryly.

"And nothin' happened here to-day?"

"Nothin' to speak of. Nothin' except that the French language has got awful popular around these parts. Damned if you ain't got to learn it before you got a chance to be elected again, sheriff."

"Who made it fashionable?" asked the sheriff, resigning his last effort to extract the direct statement of the truth from his old friend, and settling back in his chair to puff at his cigar.

"Yarnell done the most for makin' it popular," said the host thoughtfully.

"Him! He couldn't talk—"

"Couldn't he? He was talkin' it to a hoss, sheriff, before he got through. That was how fast he learned!"

"I'm a doggone patient man, Pearson."

"I'm tellin' you facts. I seen Yarnell bowin' to that hoss, too."

"He was drunk, eh?"

"No, he was scared."

The sheriff grew very quiet. "Go on," he said gently. "Who taught him French?"

"A kid dressed up like a sideshow in a circus. He looked like a picture. I expected to see the colors start runnin' when I looked at him out there in the sun. Well, he taught Yarnell French."

"Did he get Yarnell covered first, when Frank wasn't lookin'?"

"He didn't do nothin' but shoot the holster out of Frank's hand," said the host with elaborate carelessness.

There was a pause, through which the pleasant voice of a singer was heard from Alvarez' backyard, in a carol, low-pitched, impassioned of rhythm.

"Was there a square break?" asked Walter Long reverently.

"Yarnell had a mite the start," the host replied.

The sheriff took off his hat and began to fan himself hard.

"And Sladen?" said he.

"He got his wrist all bruised so mighty bad that he couldn't handle a gun."

"Fall offn his hoss?"

"Nope, a gent fell onto him."

"The devil! Who was it?"

"This same young feller that was dressed up so pretty."

Walter Long started to his feet.

26

"A sort of a pretty-lookin' gent?" he asked.

"Hey. Walt, you don't know nothin' about him, do you?"

"Not much more'n twenty, to look at him? Made mighty slick all over?"

"Walt, for heaven's sake, tell me who he is!"

"Where is he?"

"Will you tell me first?"

"Lemme locate where he is; sure I'll tell you."

"Right over yonder in Alvarez' backyard yappin' at Alicia with all the other gals in town bustin' their hearts and strainin' their ears to make out what he's hollerin' to her!"

The sheriff started for the door.

"Walt, you swore—you gave me your promise that—"

But Walter Long disengaged himself and started down the steps and across the street. He rounded the side of the Alvarez house; he went down the long dobe wall. At the rear gate, he looked over into the garden itself.

It was a tender scene. The old duenna sat fumbling with her knitting needles far in the gloom; upon the bench beside the little central pool, so still now that it showed all the small, bright faces of the stars, sat Alicia with her head thrown back to heaven; while, seated at her feet, with his head pillowed on her lap, strumming the guitar and singing up to her, lay the shadowy form of a man of whom nothing could be made out plainly except the glimmer of a crimson band around his hips.

"Slim Jim!" called the sheriff.

It was as though he had touched a spring. There was only a brief and discordant jarring of the string of the guitar as the shadow at the feet of the girl slipped into the shrubbery of the garden.

Poor Alicia, so suddenly deserted and dragged down from the balmy mist of the stars, leaped up with a frightened cry and fled to the house.

27

The sheriff regarded this sudden alteration with a mingling of concern and amusement. He paused for a moment to consider what he should do next, but before he could make up his mind a needle point pricked the skin of his back.

He whirled around and found the dull glimmer of the knife presented at his belly. It was the man of shadow, with the crimson sash around his hips.

"What fat fool," said the youngster, "is this? Who are you, my big friend, and who taught you to call me Slim Jim?"

The sheriff bit his lip. His position could not be called dignified, neither was it stimulating in a pleasant way.

"Take that knife out of my stomach," he growled presently. "You've had your fun for to-day, I guess!"

At this Jingle stepped instantly back.

"I think," said he, "that is the one thing in the world which completely upsets me. May I ask where you picked up that name?"

"Young man, it ain't for you to ask questions; your part is to answer 'em. Might I ask what you're doin' makin' trouble in this part of the country?"

"You knew me in Oklahoma, then, last month?"

"I've follered you on the map. I was hopin' that the bad news might not come this way. I follered you ever since I heard about the lightnin' flash that busted old Si Morris on the head over in—"

"I hate gossip!" Jingle interposed sharply.

"Sure," said Walter Long. "That ain't necessary. What I want to do is to find out how long you gonna be in these here parts?"

"From present indications," said Jingle, "I shall stay here quite a time. The weather seems just pleasantly warm and the scenery is beautiful."

"She'll make you a mess of trouble," said the sheriff vaguely. "What I'd aim to do if I was you, old-timer,

28

would be to hop onto a hoss and float right on out of this here Gloryville."

"Thanks," the youth remarked noncommittally. "I'll give that a thought, sir."

"I hoped," declared the sheriff, "that this here day was goin' to be half bad and half good. I thought it was gonna bring the end to Yarnell or Sladen—one of them two. And I thought that the good'd be balanced by me havin' to take bad news to the finest gent that ever stepped in these parts. Now I see that it's all bad."

"Who," asked Jingle, "is the finest man?"

"A gent you might of heard of, even pretty far away. His name is Henry A. Swain. They've busted the poor feller at last!"

"Swain?" said Jingle. "How did they break him?"

"I don't answer no questions on that," said the sheriff. "It's all private. It'll be public too soon, at that!"

"Swain?" went on Jingle in thought. "That the fellow who rides in an English saddle and looks as if he were about to fall off every step or two."

"Him? As good a hossman as ever I seen!"

"I remember him very well, now. His daughter was with him. The girl with the foolish look, you know."

At that, Walter Long snorted loudly.

"I wish to heaven," said he, "that the country was plumb full of foolish looks, because then we'd—"

"What?" asked Jingle calmly as the other fumbled for words.

"Beat the world, young man!"

"Well," mused Jingle, "when a man blunders he has to pay the penalty of his mistake."

"Is bein' robbed a blunder?" thundered the sheriff. "Is that the fault of poor Swain?"

And he stamped off down the alley, muttering to himself.

Despite the sheriff's unwillingness to talk, Mr. Jingle

29

had learned enough about the posture of Swain's affairs to have contented most men, but his curiosity on this point was insatiable. He therefore turned himself into a shadow which flitted along unobserved in the rear of Walter Long until that worthy upholder of the law reached almost the western end of the village street and turned in toward a little house which was defended from the roadway by two or three thirsty trees and a wretched semblance of a garden.

The light from the front room shone through an open window, for the night was warm, and Mr. Jingle, having crossed the veranda with a noiseless step after the sheriff entered the house, ensconced himself at the window where he could see and hear all that passed in the room.

There was enough to cause his large eyes to gleam with pleasure like a cat's in the dark when it sees prey —for in a chair sat Henry Swain and near him was his daughter. They arose to greet the sheriff who entered wiping his brow on which the sweatband of the hat had marked a crimson streak.

A pair of cowpunchers raced their horses with whoops down the street at this moment, and when Jingle looked back after a glance toward their forms as they flashed through a dim shaft of lamplight, the trio in the room were seated again.

"I brought Peggy in," said Mr. Swain. "I want her to hear everything. I want her to understand what has happened, with you standing by to confirm it."

Walter Long sighed and nodded.

"But first," continued Swain, "let me have the bad news, because I see that is what you have brought."

Mr. Long cleared his throat and looked about him, but in the silence there was nothing to help him except the clock on the mantelpiece ticking out the seconds.

"I'd have banked on old Mat Longacre," he said drearily. "Him and me was bunkies. That's how thick we was."

Swain agreed with a murmur; he had heard of their companionship.

"Well," sighed the sheriff, "the turns I've done for Longacre would have filled a book, and, the way I figured, he couldn't refuse me the first favor I asked him. I sat down and wrote it all out mighty careful. Yes, sir, I spent a whole day composin' that letter. I showed him how things was fixed with you and how them skunks— I beg your pardon, Miss Peggy—had stuck you up.

"I told him what you needed and I give him my word, on the honor of a gent that had ought to know something about ranchin', that it wasn't your fault. I told him all you needed was something that he wouldn't miss out of his millions. And he has got millions!"

"I understand that he has, in fact."

"Sure. They dug gold like dirt in the old Shawnee. But here's the answer that come back. He says—doggone me if I can read it, it makes me so mad. Mr. Swain, you have a look at it, will you?"

Henry Swain took the proffered envelope and opened the sheet which it contained.

"Typewrote, too," pointed out the sheriff. "Too proud to write a letter to an old friend with his own fist!"

" 'My dear Walter Long—' " began Swain, reading.

"Will you hark at that?" barked Walter Long. "My dear Walter Long! Hell's teeth! I been 'Walt' or 'Fatty' to him for night onto twenty year. Swain, what does New York do to men?"

"Poisons them," said Swain gently. "A very slow, painless poison which operates with great sureness. I have seen fine fellows go there and within three years become dead souls in healthy bodies."

He continued the epistle:

My dear Walter Long:
    I have read your letter with great care concerning

31

the unfortunate dilemma of the certain Mr. Swain of whom you speak, but with whom I am unfortunately not acquainted.

"It ain't Mat Longacre," raged the sheriff, beating a fat hand upon a fatter knee. "He ain't got them words. Not unless he borrowed 'em from one of his hired men." Swain continued, reading carefully.

However, I examined all that you have to say about his talents as a rancher. I can hardly agree with you that a man may be robbed of his water rights against his will. You will pardon me for saying that such a thing appears to me like a complete lack of foresight. Certainly, in a similar case, I believe that I should have made sure of water before I began raising cattle.

You tell me that Mr. Swain, when he bought his properties, had a word-of-mouth assurance that he would have the free usage of the water of the adjoining property, where there is more water than can be handled. Perhaps that word-of-mouth agreement might be the basis of a suit, to which I strongly advise Mr. Swain to proceed.

In the meantime, it is quite understandable to me that his ranch is in danger of becoming valueless. If he cannot secure the other adjoining property where he is now getting water for his cows, he is lost and will be completely landlocked. In that case, Mr. Gorman can buy him in for whatever he sees fit to pay, which will probably be a tenth part of what the property is worth.

I assure you that if I had at my disposal and—

"There's the catch," groaned Walter Long. "If he had at his disposal—him with all his millions! Why doggone me if I don't want to take a gun and go after him!"

I assure you that if I had at my disposal enough cash to buy the Lewis Solway place and so secure Mr. Swain, for the sake of our old and valued friendship, my dear Walter—

"Wait," gasped the sheriff, "it sort of gags me to hear that kind of talk!"

Mr. Swain continued to read:

for the sake of our old and valued friendship, my dear Walter, over many pleasant years, I should be more than delighted to close the deal at once and turn over the place to Mr. Swain, whose note would be ample security for me. But as matters stand, I find after a most diligent inquiry that my various properties are so tied up that the disposal of any of them is impossible except at an unthinkable sacrifice, and since I have not the requisite amount of cash on hand, I am compelled to my intense regret to inform you that I am incapable of meeting your request.

Mr. Swain folded the letter, creased it with much deliberation, replaced it in the envelope and handed it back to the sheriff without looking up.

"After all," he said, "it would have been a very great deal to expect. I was very foolish to put any trust in the idea. However, I thank you with all my heart, Long, for your great good will to us."

"I understand," Peggy said, "how Mr. Gorman shut you away from water, but I don't see why you can't keep on using dear old Mr. Solway's water. There's oceans of it; and he loves to do you the good turn."

"Dear old Mr. Solway," said her father a little bitterly, "has his back against the wall. He has piled up more debts than he has dollars since his boy died. Now he has to sell at the very reasonable figure of sixty-five thousand dollars. And there is no one in the market for the place except Hugh Gorman. Of course, if Gorman gets the place, the malice which has made him cut me off from water before will make him do it again; besides, when he has me completely surrounded, as Mr. Longacre plainly saw, Mr. Gorman can buy in my place for a song. It will be valueless to any one but to him.

"That's his plan. He picks up the work of my life for nothing, wrecks me and goes merrily on his way. I have talked to Solway. The old fellow has a heart of gold. He offered to hold out as long as he could, hoping that I could manage to raise the money. But when the last calf crop turned out such a bad one, and when blackleg hit me so hard last year, Solway saw that there was not much use in waiting longer.

"He had to set a date. And his date is the first of next month. That is to say, three weeks or thereabouts from to-day! If I can raise sixty-five thousand dollars by that time, all will be well; if not, Gorman gets the Solway place and my throat is cut."

He sat back in his chair with a sick grimace.

"But surely," cried Peggy Swain, catching at the first hope like a true woman, "you can borrow the money. Your ranch is worth a lot more than that!"

"It has a rather heavy mortgage against it already. But still it's worth a very great deal more than that. However, most banks have no faith in this locality. There have been too many droughts here and too many ranchers have failed in this section before. The only bank that could put any trust in such a loan would be some one near the place; in other words, the Loughbury Bank is the only one."

"And won't they do it?"

"The joker in that hand is that Hugh Gorman is the president of the Loughbury Bank. And so that gate is closed upon us. In fact, Peggy dear, there is only one

34

way to look at the matter. We must face the brutal facts in the case. In three weeks from to-day we will have to face a sale which cannot be consummated for even the value of the first mortgage. And from that moment we shall have to begin all over again."

"What of that?" cried Peggy, lifting her fine head. "Oh, dad, I can work. I *will* work!"

"What of that?" echoed the rancher sadly. "Why, it only means that twenty years of work are snuffed out. Twenty years—twenty years! The space of your life—and a little bit more!"

5

Off the eastern mountainside the voice rolled down on Gloryville, a bass voice so tremendous that one could not gauge the distance of the singer. Sometimes the thunder of his tones rang and rolled as though he had already entered the main street of the town. Sometimes it boomed far away, the words half lost:

> *Down by the river they was singin' like a bell,*
> *El Cantor and Little Samuel.*
> *Down by the Rio they heard 'em in the dark*
> *Singin' like a thrush and a meadow lark;*
> *Down by the Rio they looked for 'em at dawn,*
> *But the singin' was over, the singers was gone;*
> *Down by the Rio they didn't leave no track—*
> *All the señoritas there now is wearin' black,*

Waitin' and sighin' and wishin' 'em well,
El Cantor and Little Samuel.

Here the song and the singer plainly entered the village, for the last line was deep-rolling thunder through the street. To doors and windows came the population of the town and waited. And they saw a strange picture, by glimpses, until at last it approached the hotel, with the singer still bellowing.

Before him herded no fewer than four big pack mules, each loaded with a tremendous mound, and as they scatteringly made for the watering troughs and buried their muzzles in the water inches deep above the nostrils, attention could be given to the master of the train.

This was an immense black man who stood at least eight inches above the romantic height of the perfect six feet. He was proportioned in accordance with this height. The tall mules and their lofty loads, contrasted with this ebony hero, seemed like pigmy burros.

His enormous frame was surmounted by a head hideous enough to have supplied a thousand children with nightmares. The mouth was as vast as a caricature. The flattened nose was furnished with nostrils which habitually flared wide. The eyes were remarkably small, but as bright and active as the eyes of a wild boar.

His costume was as astonishing as his bulk and his countenance. The immense feet of this giant were incased in red morocco boots which would have come to the knees of a normal man and which rose high up the swelling calf of the black. Into the tops of the boots disappeared trousers of what appeared to be whipcord, but dyed jetty black, perhaps for the sake of setting off the crimson of the boots and the great silver conchos that ran from hip to knee.

The enormous torso was incased, first of all, in a Mexican jacket which was stiffened with silver thread and gold braid and which yawned open in the front to expose a shirt of rich silk of the purest and most vibrating sky blue. A broad white leather belt of fine goatskin girt the waist of this gay monster, and out of white goatskin holsters peeped the ebony butts of two large revolvers, made to match the size of the wearer, and therefore almost as large as carbines. All of this finery, at last, was topped by a great Mexican sombrero, glittering and weighted with metal work.

The black paused in the light so that the spectators could look their fill upon him. Then he advanced to the edge of the veranda.

"What might the name of this here town be, strangers?" he asked genially.

"This here is Gloryville. What might your name be, stranger?"

"Me? I'm Little Samuel."

"Hell, man, you ain't him you been singing about?"

"Could you think of somethin' better for singin' about, honey?" asked the great giant.

Across an incredible space, he stretched his arm and drew the questioner near. This was a stalwart rancher well above six feet himself, but when he was close to the superhuman shoulders of Little Samuel, he was in bulk like a child beside a man.

"Besides," said Little Samuel, "swearin' ain't a habit that's good for youngsters. It's best for growed up men."

With this, he released the prisoner and turned to the string of mules, which were lifting dripping heads from the troughs by this time.

Out of the dark of the veranda a question drifted toward him through the warm night.

"What might you be doing with all them packs, Sam?"

"My name is Sam-u-el!" pronounced the big man. "Them first three mules has got the clothes of my boss. That's El Cantor."

37

"His clothes!" shouted an incredulous voice from among the listeners. "What is he? A peddler?"

"No," Little Samuel replied, rolling his glistening eyes toward the last speaker. "He's a gen'l'man."

"What's on the fourth mule, Samuel? Your provisions and cookin' things?"

"On that there fourth mule is all of my clothes," said Little Samuel.

It brought a groan of disbelief from the listeners, and then a ready chuckle. Mirth is a rare flower in the desert, and these people were ready to be amused.

"Maybe you-all live on cactus and hope, Samuel?"

"We-all live on salt and gunpowder," Samuel retorted, and strode off leading his mules toward the stables while he raised his voice again in thundering music.

The song rolled away into the distance toward the stables, and still roared obscurely there, while the astonished men on the veranda of the hotel gaped at one another in amazement.

"Who is El Cantor?"

"That means The Singer," said another, who knew Spanish. "Maybe he's talkin' about himself?"

"Nope. He sings about himself, and he calls himself Little Samuel. This El Cantor, maybe he's another singer?"

In the meantime, Little Samuel came back into the hotel bearing upon his back an entire mule pack. His huge voice summoned the proprietor, and they went up the stairs together. At the head of the stairs, Little Samuel deposited his burden with a heavy thud that jarred the entire building.

"Now," said he, "we'll have a look at these rooms. It ain't much of a town nor much of a hotel for El Cantor to be stayin' in, but what they is of it, he's got to have the best."

The proprietor grunted. He was not one to have endured such talk from an ordinary person, but from no viewpoint could Little Samuel be considered ordinary.

"About beds," said he, "I dunno that we got any calculated for you, young man."

"A floor will do for me," Little Samuel explained. "I carry my cushions along with me." And he bestowed a huge smile upon Hen Pearson.

To the first room shown him by Pearson he gave the sole comment of a grunt. To the second he shrugged his shoulders. Finally he decided upon three chambers.

"Three?" muttered Hen Pearson. "But what'll you do with the odd one?"

"A bedroom, a room for the packs, and a room for El Cantor to sit in," said he.

So the three best rooms of the hotel were engaged, all in a row across the front of the second story of the building. And Hen Pearson went down to take the strange news to the men of the veranda. They listened to him with much amusement and wonder, which was interrupted by the musical murmuring of litttle bells down the street.

"Jingle Bells is comin'," said someone, and there was an expectant stir.

The sound of the bells increased. The form of the red bay horse flashed through the light of the hotel's great lamp, and Jingle Bells disappeared around the corner of the building toward the stables. A moment later the building was shaken by the weight of a tremendous footfall descending down the stairs, then the bellow of Little Samuel sounded in the rear of the hotel.

"By Jove!" said some one. "This Jingle Bells is a singin' man. *He's* El Cantor!"

And so he was. They spied upon the pair from a distance, and they learned many strange things. They saw the giant unsaddle the horse of Jingle Bells, they saw him advance toward the hotel walking beside the slender form of that gunfighter who looked childishly small in comparison.

Up the stairs they went together and entered the reserved rooms. There could be no doubt about it. This was El Cantor. Afterward they spied as closely as they could, but there was little they could learn.

Later, a banjo thrummed strongly and the bull-bass of the giant rolled forth a new ballad:

> *How does the eagle ride the air?*
> *So rides El Cantor!*
> *How does the wolf—*

A smaller voice interrupted. The giant ceased his thundering. And the entire hotel heard the quiet tones of Jingle Bells saying: "Your voice is like the bray of a mule. Be quiet, Samuel. This is not the desert, but a room."

6

When Jingle Bells appeared the next morning, riding Monsieur le Duc, he was so changed that the people of the town could hardly recognize him.

His Mexican trappings were gone. He was dressed in riding breeches, leather boots with softly wrinkled tops, plain steel spurs, a most conservative jacket, and a derby hat. Instead of the magnificent Spanish saddle, loaded with metal work, there was a little English pigskin hunting saddle, rubbed a rich brown-black by many applications of saddle soap.

There could not have been an outfit more jarring to the eye of the conservative cattleman than this. By contrast, the flaring clothes of the day before were ordinary and appropriate. This was a costume which would be infinitely more stared at, from the soft, shiny boots to that last graceful touch of the colorful little bow tie.

It was still well before the prime of the day when Jingle Bells came to the Swain ranch. From the hill before he reached it, he could read the story of the panorama.

All about him was a rolling country, covered now with brown, sun-cured gramma grass, the best cattle feed in the world, but as far as his eye could sweep from that high place, which was as far as a chasing hawk could wing in half an hour, he could see only one source of water, which was a meandering little yellow stream in the distance, turning twice and again into pools of some size. If a rancher were shut off from that water, he was indeed damned!

Jingle Bells considered this matter with an eye for the strategically important points. Then he went on to what had been described to him in Gloryville as the house of Henry A. Swain.

It was a rich man's home. The price of more than one prosperous farm must have been expended to raise those long, low walls of thick brick and dobe, to tile that red roof, to plant and tend that wide-sweeping garden which circled the building. All the actual ranch buildings which had to do with the work of the farm were carefully secluded. Jingle Bells marked their pointed roofs putting up above the rim of an adjacent hollow.

Then he went on to the entrance to the patio, left Monsieur le Duc outside at the hitching rack, and was about to enter the patio itself when the very person

41

whom he had come to see stood before him at the arched entrance. It was fair Peggy Swain, smiling a good morning to him. No matter what disastrous news she had heard the evening before, it had not robbed her of any sleep. She was as fresh as a pansy, and as bright.

"I watched you coming," she said. "That horse is a lovely beast!"

"Monsieur le Duc," Jingle Bells explained, "has not yet seen you. But when he does, I'm sure that he'll have some sort of a greeting—a bow, perhaps."

No one could have said that there was the slightest additional emphasis upon that word, but Monsieur at once lowered his head until the mane flicked the dust. Then he looked up again with pricking ears, a picture so beautiful that the girl cried out softly.

"How did you train him?" she asked.

"With a whip, of course," Jingle Bells replied. "One needs a whip for most difficult things, you know."

At this, she met his eyes a little diffidently. He was so young, so handsome, so deliberately the master of himself that it made his cruelty a dreadful thing.

And a fierce desire arose in her to crush this fellow in some manner—she knew not how. To best him utterly, and make him sue for mercy. It would be very pleasant to do such a thing with so proud a peer!

"You are traveling a long distance, I suppose," she said coldly, "or you would never have made such an early start?"

"On the contrary," he replied. "I always make an early start. The night and the morning and the evening— they are worth something, but the heart of the day is a blank, for me. It was business that brought me out here this morning."

"Oh," said she without enthusiasm, and waited, making no effort to draw him out. All this time she was studying him, telling herself that she had never met a man whom she liked so little. She was accustomed, most of all, to modest young men, who were very much abashed in her presence, no matter how bold they might be among others.

But this slender youth was as much at ease as though she was a rose bush, or any other inanimate, attractive thing. In just the same fashion did he eye her.

"It has to do," said Jingle Bells, "with your father's difficulty."

She flushed quickly and hotly at this.

"I suppose the town is talking of that?" she asked.

He waved a reassuring hand which made her hate him more than ever. Certainly he was the right exemplification of self-esteem.

"The town is not talking," he explained. "But I have means of gaining private information. Strictly private, Miss Swain."

She felt, at that moment, that she would be glad to see the earth swallow the impertinent wretch.

"If you have business with my father," she said, "you had better find him. I think he's in the house."

"I haven't any business with your father," he assured her quickly. "Only with you, Miss Swain."

"I hardly understand," said she, and she eyed him up and down with an icy hauteur which she had seen other women use, but which she had never donned before in person. The result was not what she could have desired.

The impossible Jingle Bells simply smiled and even nodded a little, as if he approved of the spirit which made her act in this fashion. He was like a master of deportment, correcting her or grading her efforts. Peggy Swain grew more and more angry.

"Of course not," Jingle Bells agreed, "I could hardly expect you to understand."

"Besides," said she stiffly, "I regret that this is a busy morning and—"

43

"Not at all," said he, and smiled in the same maddening and superior fashion again. "This business of mine is so important that I know you'll be glad to postpone everything else."

"You are sure?" she inquired, growing a darker red in her anger.

"Of course. Because, you see, I've come to inquire if I may not have the privilege of advancing the money in which your father stands in need—the sixty-five thousand dollars, you know."

She was so angered that even her astonishment did not equal the heat of her temper. But although she stared fixedly at him, she had to admit that there was no insolent triumph in his eyes. He merely had stated a fact; she had to submit to its importance.

"My father," said she, "will of course be delighted and surprised!"

"He is not to hear of it, however," Jingle Bells announced. "Not at present, at least. He has not the sort of security that I want."

"What?" cried she. "Isn't this ranch—"

He made a little gesture which interrupted her.

"A ranch is all very well, of course. But what in the world could I do with one?"

"I suppose," said she coldly, "that you have never worked on one?"

"Never," he replied. "I've never believed in work, you know. It gives one so many monotonous hours."

She gritted her teeth at this superb asininity.

"Perhaps," she remarked choking. "In the meantime, if you do not consider the ranch as security, I hardly see what there is on which you can risk the money you propose to advance. Unless, perhaps, you're interested in the house?"

She was of two minds. The first was to send him scurrying about his business with a well-directed sarcasm or

44

two, such as the most gently reared girl knows well how to aim. The second thought was that, no matter what she did, she must not imperil the slight chance that this fellow actually had a serious intention or power of being of help to her distracted father.

He did not answer for a moment, and his eye grew cold and steady on her.

"Well?" she asked.

"I simply want to know what you would do for your father?"

"Anything! My life!"

"I thought so. And that's exactly it. That's the security that I want."

She smiled vaguely at him.

"I'm trying to understand."

"To me," he explained, in a most businesslike fashion, "you represent a security worth at least sixty-five thousand dollars. Are you willing, then, to let me consider you in that light?

"Will you mortgage yourself for the sum of sixty-five thousand dollars, payable in thirty days, or at the end of that time, redeemable by the deed of yourself to me by the act of marriage?"

Somewhere out of the distant past she could remember a high-pitched, almost a wailing voice which had passed up and down a street—perhaps in some village, perhaps in a city—she could not remember, except that it was in her childhood. And plainly, plainly the words had rung in her ears, because there was a sinister ring in them, it had seemed to her.

"Cash for old clothes! New dollars for old clothes! From a bridal gown to a pair of shoes, cash for old clothes; cash, cash for old clothes!"

That voice, in her childhood, had made her look down at the pretty frock she was wearing and wonder how many months it would be before the smudging fingers

45

of the peddler tried its texture and offered a price.

And now, listening to this stranger talking, the old idea came back to her. She was looking down to herself, to her very soul. Here was a thumb trying the texture of her nature, putting a price upon it, callously, coldly, offering money for a soul if she cared to cast it away.

"Oh!" exclaimed Margaret Swain, "what manner of man are you?"

Her sneer did not seem to affect the heartless lightness of his manner in the slightest degree. He merely smiled on her more boldly than ever.

"I am a business man," said he. "I do odd jobs here and there. Sometimes, and this may really amuse you, I look upon myself as a sort of social surgeon. I cut away unneccssary limbs; I remove people who are blocking the now of the world's life. I hope that you are able to follow me?"

"Do you mean," asked the girl shuddering, "that you actually are boasting that you kill? And that you take money for it?"

"There is pay of varying kinds," said the youth. "Some will accept nothing except hard cash. But there are others, like myself, who work by a system of exchange. For me, a mere look at a beautiful horse means a great deal more, perhaps, than a day's ride on a poor nag or the ownership of such a brute; the touch of silk under the finger tips is as delightful when the silk belongs to another as when it belongs to oneself; and as for hired murdering, that would take away the pleasure of destruction.

"However," he added with a smile, "you must not take what I have been saying too seriously. I am a very gentle person, I assure you. Many of my most intimate friends have never heard me so much as raise my voice!"

She could well believe him. There was a feline suppleness about his manner and the very tones in which

46

he spoke. Even the grace of his gestures appeared to her well-nigh dangerous. Then she felt that she could have endured the frown of another person with much greater ease than she could have withstood the smile of this beautiful devil.

Tenderness swam into his eyes as he looked upon her, and Margaret shuddered. The fiend was wooing her!

"Do I know your name?" she asked.

"I am John Albert."

"Mr. John Albert, you have offered sixty-five thousand dollars; and apparently you are serious. You will give me sixty-five thousand dollars for myself?"

"My dear Miss Swain, if you will pardon me for being so frank, let me point out that I am not asking for your soul. I am asking you to marry me."

"And what will you call that but a sale of the soul?" she asked.

"If I were to pay ten millions," he said, "I could not buy your love."

"You could not," she agreed. "And I hardly see in what manner—"

"I can get the value of my money?"

"That is it!"

At this, he tilted back that graceful head of his. It was like the swaying of a flower on a stalk, to use a very old simile. He laughed, and as he laughed she cringed before him.

"I have no fear of that," he said. "I am paying sixty-five thousand dollars, mademoiselle, for possession. After you are mine, I will guarantee that the rest will follow."

To this she could return no answer, for she knew that if she ventured further speech at that moment she would lose control of herself and break out into a rage of scorn and of detestation. And that sharp-witted Señor Jingle Bells seemed to read her mind. He remained as matter

47

of fact, as businesslike, as he had been from the first of the affair.

Now he took out a slip of paper and offered it to her. She read aloud slowly, word by word:

I, Margaret Swain, promise to become the wife of John Albert upon the payment by him to me of the sum of sixty-five thousand dollars.

She had read of terror freezing the blood. Now a chill of exquisite horror traveled through her body. What she wanted to do, first of all, was to flee with all her might.

She remembered suddenly that she was a Swain, and that a Swain cannot run away like a frightened child. So she took herself in hand with an iron grip. There was not a single tremor of her voice when she spoke: "This is wrong."

"In what way?"

"I promise to go through the marriage ceremony, I do not promise to become your wife."

"Ah?" said he. And he raised his eyebrows at her, and looked so perfectly the part of one of those supercilious gentry of the eighteenth century, those perfumed, dueling exquisites, that her breath and her heart failed her. "It will do very well," he announced at last. "I desire only that you assume the name, Miss Swain."

She could see, however, a faint flush forming on his brow and a pallor on his cheek. He was furiously angry. There was no doubt of that. And his passion filled her with a strange terror and a stranger joy, as though she were watching a wicked black leopard lashing its silken flanks with an ominous tail.

He made the change on the paper.

"According to this," said she, "there is no time set. You might come at any time with an offer of sixty-five

48

thousand dollars. And I should have to marry you."

"We will change it, of course, in any reasonable way that you wish."

"Set a time limit. Naturally, I won't wish to borrow the money from you—"

"The wrong term, Miss Swain. It is a sale, not a loan."

She flushed in spite of herself. It was not so much his words. It was the insufferable insolence of his smile, and his way of looking her up and down.

"We will change it this way."

She turned the paper over, took a fountain pen from his hand and wrote:

> I, Margaret Swain, promise to have the wedding ceremony performed between myself and John Albert, if at any time within the next twenty-seven days I ask and receive from him the sum of sixty-five thousand dollars.
>
> MARGARET SWAIN.

She offered him the document and he perused it carefully. Then he nodded, folded the paper and put it in his pocket.

"You still hope that you may get the money from some one else," he observed.

"Certainly," she replied. "I am not without friends."

"Of course not," said he. "I wish you every manner of luck with them."

"You are very kind," Peggy remarked spitefully. Then in an outburst of frankness and of anger she added: "Do you realize that, no matter what ceremony I pass through, I would never be your *wife*? Do you realize that you are paying for a name only?"

He bowed to her, so formally and so deeply that she thought again of a long-dead century.

"I understand entirely," he answered.

49

"Then you will be very foolish——"

"You really do not understand," said he, with his calm smile of self-content which she had come to hate so much already. "I am a gambler. I love a long chance. And this chance, I assure you, is not the longest that I have ever taken."

It was such a whiplash stroke that she could not help stamping her foot, although she regretted that childish outburst at once.

"Have you any command for me?" he asked.

"None!"

He bowed to her again, leaped into the saddle on the blood-bay stallion and was suddenly gone down the road. What a picture they made together, this horse and man! She watched with a sort of soaring joy in her heart, quite divorced from all the thought of John Albert as a man. He was simply part of a beautiful picture.

He reached the top of the nearest hill and, swinging off his hat, turned and waved to her again, before he shot over the edge of the eminence and dropped into invisibility beyond.

At that she flushed again. How perfectly egotistical he was to have dreamed she would be waiting there in front of the house to see the wave of his hat before he went out of view! And how much she would have given if, when he turned, he had had the chagrin of finding that not a single eye was resting upon him!

7

When John Albert had ended his repast he sat back with a cup of coffee in his hand and a long Egyptian cigarette between his thin fingers, blowing forth clouds of smoke, watching them form milk-white in the lamplight and turn to ghosts in the upper darkness of the room. He had barely tasted small portions of the food, which Samuel had fixed with joyous care.

The big servant devoured all that was left, as flame devours a forest. In a trice the great work was ended. There remained nothing but the polished dishes. To the last roll of bread, to the last shred of meat, all was gone, and Little Samuel rolled his eyes from side to side, desiring more.

Then John Albert spoke.

"Bring me the mail," said he. "Bring me all the letters."

They were brought—a half dozen envelopes. He sorted them over one by one. Finally, one addressed in a bold but feminine script held his eye. While he regarded it he said dreamily: "How did you get them?"

"That was easy," said Little Samuel, making himself a cigarette with a single twist of his thick fingers and then wafting forth immense clouds of smoke. "That was easy, El Cantor. I watched them. They take all the mail from the ranch to the mail box at the end of the day. The postmaster comes for it in the middle of the next morning."

El Cantor again regarded the envelope which he had chosen from the group. It was addressed to Hugh Nichols, Esq., in New York.

"Open this," said he to Little Samuel, handing him

51

the letter. "Open it, you scoundrel, so that a detective working with a microscope could never dream that it had been touched between she who wrote it and he who will receive it."

Little Samuel took the letter, regarded it for a moment, and then set to work at once. From some luggage in the corner of the room he produced a small alcohol lamp and a tiny copper kettle. This latter was presently boiling over the blue flame and in the steam which issued forth, he held the envelope until the mucilage was moistened through, the paper was soaked, and the flap came easily open at the deft touch of his fingers.

And in this work, for all the vastness of his hands, their touch was as delicate as the touch of a great surgeon. Then he dried the moist paper so that there was no chance that it might touch the contents of the envelope. Finally he drew forth a sheet of stiff paper and presented it to the master.

"Clear out the rubbish," said El Cantor, and while Little Samuel bore forth the tray, with a last curious side glance at the reader, John Albert was deep in the contents of the letter.

Whatever the weight of the contents, it had been written with a careless speed, the pen sweeping hastily along. And this is what he read:

DEAR HUGH:

I have often told you that you are like my father. Big like him, and strong like him, and brave like him. And when I told you that I wanted you to come West to our place some day, I hoped it would be simply for a hunting trip, and as good a time as we could give you. For I have heard you say, often, how much you love to hunt.

Partly I used to want you to come because I knew that you and dad would love each other, being both such manly men. But now all of this is changed, on dad's side, at least. He has received a crushing blow. He goes about the house like a dazed man.

And this is the trouble. He has been hedged in by an unscrupulous neighbor, a rancher who hates him, and who now has it in his power, unless something should be done within the next three weeks, to destroy all the work of dad's life. We should be able to get a loan, but the only bank in this district is under the influence of dad's enemy. There is nothing for him to do except to look abroad. And he doesn't know where to look. He doesn't want charity, you understand. All he wants is a fighting chance, and he'll be able to repay any loan—repay what he needs within three years at the most.

Hugh, what I am asking you to do is to come to us and see the condition of the place, hear the reasons of my father, and make up your mind for yourself. The sum he needs is exactly sixty-five thousand dollars. If you care to look into a matter of that size, and if you can spend the time to come here, I cannot tell you what it will mean to us. And if it were in my power to reward you, Heaven knows that there is nothing I wouldn't do.

If you can't come and if the whole matter is impossible to you, say so frankly, but say so by wire, for I shall be in the most heartbreaking suspense until I hear from you.

Margaret Swain.

From the third careful reading of this manuscript El Cantor looked up, disturbed by the feeling that a shadow had fallen across him, and he saw above him the shadowy bulk and the glittering eyes of Little Samuel.

"Seal this again," said he, and handed the letter to Little Samuel.

And Little Samuel, lighting his alcohol lamp again, took care to read the letter for himself with as much care, surely, as his master had used. After which he grinned immensely out of the darkness and licked his lips again as if he had but just finished another meal.

"Now, as to Minter," El Cantor said. "Did you locate him?"

"I found him. He's powerful glad you-all is in these parts, boss."

"Mail that letter with the rest. Then bring Minter back to me."

Little Samuel disappeared, and El Cantor, taking up a guitar, thrummed a melody so lightly that the naked voice of the strings was heard and nothing of their metal purring or clangor. To this gentle accompaniment he sang an air exquisitely subdued, hardly louder than the strings themselves until, some minutes later, Little Samuel came in with "Chick" Minter behind him.

"Well, pal—" began Chick, but the immense hand of Littte Samuel caught at him and compelled him to silence with a single grip. And El Cantor finished his song deliberately, without haste, just as he had finished his meal. Then he said, without turning his head: "Come on over here, Minter, and sit down."

Minter, a little sullen and not a little abashed, came forward to that dim place in the room where the master was sitting.

"We haven't seen each other for some time, Chick," said Jingle Bells, without any more formal greeting and without offering to shake hands.

"About a year, I guess," said Chick, recovering heart. "Not since—"

"Right," said El Cantor. "Not since then."

The little bullnecked man stared suspiciously around him.

"Can't you talk here?" he asked. "Is these walls extra thin? Ain't Little Samuel all right?"

El Cantor did not give him enough heed to answer his question.

"You have been in Loughbury," said he.

"Yep."

"There's a bank there, Chick."

"Ah!" sighed Minter. "Ain't there, though!"

"Is it an up-to-date safe?"

"Is that the game?"

"I asked you about the safe."

"I dunno. I think it's pretty good."

"You're a disgrace to your profession, Minter. You ought to know the face and the initials of every safe in the countryside. Is that bank well guarded?"

"They keep that bank in their pocket," grumbled Minter. "They got two gunmen watchin' her every night, and during the day there's enough sawed-off shotguns lyin' around that place to blow a whole regiment of gents in the profession to hell and back."

"You're broke, Minter."

"Me? What makes you think that I am?"

"You're so civil to-night."

"I ain't so flush I could make a speech about it. Well?"

"Samuel!"

The giant had faded into the obscurity in the corner of the room. Now he developed into full view without a sound, behind the back of Minter.

"Give Chick fifty dollars," said the master.

The giant turned around. Paper was heard to rustle. He faced Minter again and handed him a small sheaf of bills.

"Is this your walkin' safe deposit?" asked the yegg.

"It is," admitted El Cantor.

"Well," said Chick, "you got a nerve to trust him!"

55

"I don't," answered the master calmly, turning with a yawn. "But I haven't quite enough money to make it worth while for Little Samuel to murder me. Otherwise he'd break my back some night—if he found his chance. Another thing—he's never quite so sure of his chance with me—eh, Samuel?"

Samuel rolled his eye in a trance of doubt. Then he decided that this was a jest and at once the twin semicircles of his teeth gleamed white in the lamp shine.

"Now, go to Loughbury, Chick," ordered El Cantor. "Come back to-morrow night. I want to know everything. The make of that safe, the amount of soup you need to blow it, and so on, down to the number of men that each of those guards have killed—on duty and off!"

"Is that all?"

"A day is a long time," said El Cantor.

"To get all *that*?"

"Certainly. Good night."

Chick Minter muttered, hesitated, and then left the room.

"Go after him," said El Cantor. "He may take it into his head to go to the sheriff's house before he goes to Loughbury."

"Well, boss?" whined Little Samuel with a deadly trace of eagerness in his voice.

"If he does, strangle him, and hide his body so that the buzzards will have a chance at it."

He opened a cigarette case, and selected a smoke, but he waited in vain for a light. Then he looked around him, but he discovered that Little Samuel had already glided softly from the room.

After that he apparently changed his mind about smoking. He crumpled the cigarette wastefully, snapped it into a corner, and went to the window. Sitting on the edge of the sill, he leaned a little into the night, holding the guitar, and his voice floated out over the night.

56

"Shut up your caterwaulin', you—" began a husky voice from the street.

That voice was rudely interrupted by the shout of a companion: "Look out, you fool, that gent that's singin' is—"

The rest of that warning was a muttering, but El Cantor was content. He smiled over his song, and, leaning against the side of the window, he let the music drift forth again, from his lips, from his throat, almost from his heart.

Then, at a pause, he waited, silent. And presently from the opposite darkness, welling up pure and small, a woman's voice answered, singing in Spanish an old air, but with the words neatly altered:

> *Oh, heart beware! The night is young.*
> *I wait, but yet wait not alone—*

El Cantor was stirred enough to slip to his feet. And as her stanza died, his answer went instantly forth:

> *Be the walls triple brass and the gates of steel,*
> *Be the guards appointed and armed,*
> *Yet at your feet before dawn I kneel,*
> *For the life of the lover is charmed.*

He turned, cast the guitar away, so that it fell upon the bed with a brief, discordant stir of strings, tossed off the kimono, slipped into a jacket, and started.

8

At the door he paused to finger for an instant the gun which hung there from a cartridge belt. But apparently he changed his mind at once, for he abandoned the revolver and rested his hand on the haft of a knife which was slipped inside the sash that girdled his waist. This was armament enough for him.

He stood for a moment, drawing himself up straight and stiff in the dark, still gripping the handle of the knife, and taking the feel of the floor through his slippers. They were made of goatskin, tough as steel and thin as paper, better than bare feet for swift and secret work. He had proved them before. In the meantime, what was that danger which Alicia warned him of if he dared to visit her through the night?

He had turned to the door again, when it opened. Little Samuel, despite his bulk, could make himself a noiseless shadow, just as the elephant, that most prodigious of beasts, can go through the dense jungle more silently than a cat. So came Little Samuel and, opening the door, stood before his master, a great shadow in which his teeth and his eyes glistened and moved.

"Where did he go?" the master demanded.

"He's still alive," answered Little Samuel significantly.

El Cantor nodded and instantly left the room. He chose to leave the hotel not by the stairs, which could be observed and his going and his coming noted. Perhaps even he, indifferent as he was to the opinion of others, might have been stirred a little if the cowpunchers of Gloryville had seen him in this outfit, which was

58

more like the costume of a stage gymnast than wearing apparel for the street.

He went through a back window of the hotel, dropped lightly to the slant roof of the kitchen, and crouched there to watch. There was plenty of noise in the street at the front of the hotel, but here all was black. The only thing that moved was a cat which leaped up to the top of a fence and glided along it, a gray splotch. Farther up, the trees spread their branches, and their blotting shadows beneath them. And beyond, the mountaintops were wedges driven high among the stars. These things he saw.

Then he dropped down to the backyard, ran past the rear of several houses, with a stealthy stride, and at length, at a place where the street was narrowest, where no one was near, he darted out and flashed across the sheltering shadows of the farther side.

A moment later he was crouched outside the garden gate of Señor Alvarez. The girl was not there in the garden by the fountain. He slipped through the gate, and then he found her. The window of her room was open.

Alicia sat inside, working in a pout at a bit of embroidery with an old withered duenna at her side. And in the shadow beneath the window was another shadow, coiled and waiting, lit with one spark dimmer than the reflection of a ray of starlight. That was the gun, or the knife, that guarded the daughter of Alvarez.

El Cantor drew himself up again, that favorite attitude of his, with the straining, mirthless smile which expressed a fierce delight, a rapture of the spirit. Then he began to work.

The walls were low and of rough masonry. He glided up the face of the house like a shadow and brought his head to the level of the flat roof.

There were chairs here, and in a corner sat the great Señor Alvarez, the rich man, himself. He was drinking tequila, smoking cigarettes of a nameless vileness, and regarding the stars above his head. Beside him was his wife, snoring, and the backs of both were turned to the adventurer.

He grinned at them again through the dark, like a lurking wolf. Then he slid across the roof and looked down over the edge. Just beneath him was the glow of the lighted window of Alicia's room, and just below the window the coiled shadow uncurved, straightened, and turned into a tall man, with a revolver in his hand which gleamed as he extended his arms to stretch. His head came above the edge of the lamplight from the room. It was crowned with a tall sombrero on which glinted metal work of yellow and white—a sufficient announcement that here was a caballero of some importance or at least of some self-esteem.

Before the long, strong arms were gathered in from the elaborate process of stretching and yawning, El Cantor resolved to act. In an instant he was dangling from the edge of the roof by his hands, looking down, aiming his fall. Then he dropped.

He who falls from a height seems to hang for an instant, almost suspended. Then a mighty hand reaches invisibly from beneath and wrenches its victim down with dizzy speed.

So fell El Cantor. And while he shot through the midspace, the luckless knight of the window, bending his head far back to make the yawn more deliciously perfect, looked up perforce, and saw the impending danger. It was a hundredth part of a second away. There was no time to stir. Only a vague sound could form itself in his throat. Then he was smitten to the ground and lay in blackness that swallowed his senses.

El Cantor knelt by him and calmly made sure that the

60

heart still beat. He himself was shaken, and he feared for a moment that he had broken the man's neck. El Cantor rarely killed if he could avoid it, for the simple reason that a slayer is building up a great balance against himself which must one day be paid; and also because murder will never be forgotten or forgiven. But a blow or a gun play is only a blow or a gun play—in a word, a game.

This man was not badly hurt, but the wind was knocked out of his lungs, and he was senseless. It would be many long seconds before he recovered. In the meantime, although the old duenna had been looking straight at the window, all had happened so quickly that she could not be sure what she had seen.

El Cantor heard her talking.

"Alicia, what was that?"

"What was what, madre?"

"At the window!"

"Well?"

"I saw his head—"

"What of that?"

"I don't know."

"Bah!" said the girl. "I am going mad."

Then El Cantor stood at the window and smiled in at her.

Even though her eyes widened and she turned pale, yet she smiled in the same instant. The old woman was speechless, and before breath came to her El Cantor was in the room and at her side. He showed her the snowy steel of his knife.

"This and your throat, mother," said he in soft, quick Spanish. "Remember! Go into the corner and turn your back. You see nothing; you hear nothing. Your brain is sleeping. But if you should weaken and remember anything at another time, and if Alvarez should learn of it, do you know what would happen? I would come to you

61

at midnight and slit your neck from ear to ear. So!"

He made an effective gesture in the air, and the aged woman cowered away from him to a corner of the room. There she was in too deadly a fear to quite turn her back. She had to keep this serpent of a man in the corner of her eye, and so she saw him take Alicia in his arms, and she heard Alicia cry: "Señor! Señor! This is using force!"

But the cry was no louder than the whisper of a bird's wing as it brushes among the flowers.

"Alicia," said he, "you have been in my heart from that first moment. I have been drinking the thought of your beauty, my bird. So—so—and so!"

She raised a hand against him. It was of no more force than the curling petal of a flower which the touch of the night is shutting and the first ray of the sun will suffice to open for the day again.

"The madre will see you!" breathed Alicia, trembling with fear and with joy.

"The duenna is blind. Tell me, child—you love me?"

"Alas, señor, it is the first time. I am afraid!"

There was a groan from the night beyond the window.

"In the name of heaven, señor—"

"In the name of heaven, confess, Alicia! I am in your heart!"

"Ah, señor, if I speak, then you will break my heart. Now go! They are coming! I am sure I heard—"

"They will not come. This is a charmed night for me, and the lives of all lovers are charmed, Alicia. Tell me three words. Speak, Alicia! You love me!"

"I love you, señor!"

"And I you. And I leave these pledges of my love—in the hollow of your throat—in the dimple of this cheek—on your lips, your sweet, soft lips, Alicia."

The duenna clutched at a string of beads which hung from her neck, but the first prayer came sidewise and confused from her lips and the second was a gibbering.

The guard outside the window groaned again and then called feebly for help. That instant, and then only, El Cantor shot through the casement, struck down the poor guard, and turned again to the girl.

"Why is this hired watchdog here?" he asked.

"My father fears you, because you sing to me," said she. "He is bringing a rich man from Mexico to marry me, oh, dearest. But you will come and take me—"

"From hell, in spite of the devil, even though he wore the name of your father. Ten thousand happy dreams!"

He stepped from the light of the window just in time to fall into the arms of two men who were rushing around the side of the house in response to the summons of the stricken watcher.

But what can even a strong man do when he is smitten upon the Adam's apple by a hand of steel, choking his breath, turning his head to fire? And what can a strong man do when he is sliced by a knife edge and blinded with spurting blood?

El Cantor leaped away from those two faithful ones with the sweet knowledge that only two in the house of Alvarez had seen his face. And one of these would never speak for love of him, and one of these would never speak for dread of him. So all was well!

In fifty seconds he was in his room at the hotel, and with a word he had set Little Samuel in furious action. It was only two minutes later that the sheriff arrived, red with haste, his hand resting on the butt of his gun.

And he found El Cantor lying back in a deep chair, smoking a Chinese pipe a full yard in length of jointed, silver-mounted bamboo stem, but with a bowl which held no more than a single pinch of fragrant, perfumed to-bacco. So he smoked steadily, slowly, inhaling every breath deep, and Little Samuel, like a priest at an altar, was devoutly filling and refilling the bowl and lighting it.

The sheriff came sweating to El Cantor. "Young man," said he, "stand up and come with me!"

"Ah," said El Cantor, "have you found out something about me?"

"You admit you got a record, then?" cried Sheriff Walter Long.

"Of course. But I hope it's fairly well concealed. But what have you found out?"

"Tonight's little job," said the sheriff. "We'll tell you the details later on."

"Nonsense," smiled El Cantor, closing his eyes again. "I have not left my room."

And the sheriff, seeing that the bluff would not work, rushed out again to get testimony. He could not scrape together enough to make a sentence out of it all. And when he questioned the duenna and Alicia, they grew indignant and denounced him to his face.

"Which proves that they're lyin'," said the sheriff to Alvarez. "Because when a woman is plumb innocent, she's always scared."

However, he had not a scruple of proof, and so El Cantor did not spend that night in the jail.

9

Until midnight the town of Loughbury, like any other healthy Western town with restless cowpunchers and eager prospectors in it, was full of life and noise. But after that, one needed action to keep one awake.

So those twin two-legged bulldogs who guarded the Loughbury Bank and drew down fat weekly pay checks from wise, cautious Mr. Gorman remained at ease until after midnight. At that time they started to walk their beats.

They began, back to back, in front of the horse shed at the rear of the bank. They passed down the alleys on either side of the Loughbury Bank, turned the front corners, passed each other, and continued around again, so that each had an alternate view of both sides of the building and what one missed the other might perceive.

There was not much danger of a miss, however. Both Rudy Michaels and Sam Jewel came out of one school, and both were hawks. It is entirely due to the foresight and the vision of Mr. Gorman that these men had been obtained. He had reasoned, with his business associates, in the following fashion: "There is only one thing which will keep a bank at night—that is not the strength of steel, but the power of vigilance exercised by two faithful men who will be sure not to overlook anything, and who will be so inured to long vigils that there is no danger that they may fall asleep. Get the men, and let the fine safes and the thick steel walls go!"

So spoke Mr. Gorman, the president, and the others said simply: "Go get two perfect men of that type, and we'll agree with you."

He lived up to his word. During his next vacation he journeyed north to shoot, and while he was in the wilds of Canada he went among that race of shrewd, patient, strong-nerved men—the trappers. Your hunter is a man of temperament. He is an artist. He lives under a tension. But your trapper is a strategist. He may have the quickest hand and the surest eye in the world, but unless he has wits, and good sound ones, he will never progress in his work.

Mr. Gorman searched among these people of the vast

65

northern forests until he found two to his liking. They resembled each other more than twin brothers. They were thin, brown-faced men with restless eyes and steady hands. They spoke seldom. They had no friends. They lived for and with their traps and their guns.

Such was Rudy Michaels; such was Sam Jewel. They were tall men. They walked habitually with long strides, flexing the knees greatly as though the heavy snowshoes were under their feet and the heavy pack were between their shoulders. It was hard to persuade them from their chosen lives, but the salary which Mr. Gorman offered was too much, and they came south. They had been on guard for eight years, and for eight years, while robbers smashed bank after bank throughout the district, the Loughbury Bank went unscathed and not a cent of its deposits was missing.

And in that war in which the battles were so far apart, so brief, so bloody, Rudy Michaels had killed no fewer than five armed thieves at the cost of two grim wounds whose scars still marked his body, and Sam Jewel had killed three men and bore five scars in his flesh. Such was their record.

Furthermore, in the town they had no friends, nor did they seek any. Neither did they fraternize with each other. Each carried in his eyes a fever of longing to be back in the northern woods in the cold and the wet and the loneliness. But each was held in a golden tether by Mr. Loughbury.

They grew more solemn, more silent, more vicious of speech and manner. For what use was there for wits in this ceaseless nightly circling of the bank? There was need of nothing, save patience and a chance to kill. It was for these chances that they waited hungrily, and with the stern endurance of starved wolves on a trail.

At the door of Sam Jewel came a knock on the afternoon of this day, just after he had wakened and his fire was kindled. He looked through a slit in the rickety wall, first of all, and he saw a slender man, very gaily dressed, smoking a fragrant, tailor-made cigarette, and with a magnificent blood-red stallion, a glorious deep bay, in the street near by.

Sam Jewel almost smiled at the sight of such childish display as golden spurs and jeweled conchos. Nevertheless, he opened the door—only a habitual crack, however. Then he waited. He hated to waste words.

"You're Mr. Michaels, aren't you?" said the young stranger with a very ingratiating smile.

Sam Jewel regarded him with a wolfish sneer.

"I ain't," said he. "I'm Jewel."

"Ah," said the youth. "Perhaps you can tell me where your boss is, then?"

"You mean Gorman?"

"Gorman? No, I mean Michaels."

Jewel opened the door to its full width. "Son," said he, "I dunno who you are or how you do your thinkin', but I'm here to state that I ain't got no boss. Gorman pays me once a week. That's all."

The handsome youth rubbed his chin and shook his head.

"Why," said he, "I understood that Michaels had killed five men and you only got rid of three, and that's why Gorman pays Michaels five dollars a week more'n he pays you, and——"

"Does he pay Michaels more?" asked Jewel softly. "More'n he pays me?"

"Why, of course. Don't you know?"

"Because he had the luck?"

"I don't know about that. Well, if you can't tell me where Michaels lives, I'll go along."

The youth with the beautiful red bay stallion disappeared; but Jewel remained in his door, staring, a long time after the horse was gone. He cooked a meal with

67

little interest; he ate it with less; and all that day he was observed to be more silent than ever, but he did not open his lips or speak a syllable until after midnight, when he and Michaels began their walk; and as they started in front of the horse shed Jewel said: "Well, boss, how's things?"

Rudy Michaels stopped and stared after the long-striding form of the other as Jewel went away on the round. It was very surprising. For eight days they had not spoken to each other. Between them words were not needed. Each could do what it was necessary to do. Each had eyes. Each despised talk.

Three times the shadows passed in their rounds. The Jewel spoke again: "I hear you're sportin' a raise in pay."

There was no answer until they passed again.

"What you mean by that, Jewel?"

"You're keepin' it dark, eh?" sneered Jewel.

The next time they passed it was in front of the woodshed. They paused as by common consent.

"What did you mean by that?" asked Michaels.

"Five dollars more a week, that's what I mean. What for? Why should Gorman give you five more?"

"Who said he did?"

"Don't lie, Michaels."

"Are you callin' me a liar?"

"Why not?"

They did not wait to draw weapons. They leaped at each other like beasts and clinched. Two pair of skill-ful fighting hands were well employed, and they were toppling toward the ground when a rope hissed softly through the air and then the noose of a lariat bit home on them and bound them helplessly face to face. A sack was cast over their heads. The rope wound again and again about them. Their feet were lashed, their hands secure.

"Now rest quiet, gents," said an immense voice, lowered until it sounded like far-humming thunder. "I'm right here with a gun to tickle your ribs. Rest quiet."

Thus were eight years of vigilance undone at a stroke.

As for El Cantor and Chick Minter, they paused only to make sure that all was well, patted Little Samuel on one muscle-cushioned shoulder, and then went into the bank.

There they worked without haste. The night was young, the task simple. No need for "soup" and its alarming noise, which would go booming through all of Loughbury. They needed only a "can opener," and when the steel bar had been at work for a scant half hour, the door of the safe was off.

They forced the drawers inside very easily, and then Chick Minter sat down cross-legged on the ground. He was in the presence of more cash than he had ever seen in the world—more than he had ever dreamed of—and he was trembling and giggling like a hysterical girl.

"We'll make the split right here!" he said. "There ain't any call to wait. We'll make the split right here. You take half, and I'll take half, and we'll blow in different directions."

He began to count out the bills with shaking fingers. How rapidly the sum mounted—what oceans of it there were! There had been great sales of cattle and of lands. The Loughbury Bank was choked with hard cash, and they could dip their hands into it is far as they wished.

Fifty, sixty, seventy thousand dollars were counted out by Chick Minter, and still he was only making a beginning in his task, when a word from El Cantor made him look up into the muzzle of a revolver held by that slender youth with dismaying steadiness.

"By heaven," breathed Chick Minter, "you're gonna croak me! You'll fry in—"

"Count off five thousand," commanded El Cantor.

It was done with stumbling fingers.

69

"Put that in your pocket. Now stand up. Listen to me, Chick. You've done your work very well, but I could have hired a dozen others who would have worked just as well. Yesterday you were broke; to-day you have five thousand iron men. That's enough. This sixty-five thousand goes to me. The rest of that coin goes back into the safe. Now, march!"

The gesture of the revolver was most eloquent, and Chick marched.

"I know," he snarled as he went. "You'll come back and sneak off the rest of that coin when I'm away."

The whisper of the master at his ear was as deadly in intent as the hiss of a cobra.

"I said the rest of the money remains in the bank!"

Chick made a gesture of despair.

"It ain't fair, pal," he whined. "It ain't fair to let all that good money go to waste like that!"

The remainder of the complaint of Chick Minter was cut short by an ominous double rap at the front door of the bank, followed by a sharp snapping sound outside the building and toward the rear, telling that Little Samuel, having given the alarm, had made haste to break for cover.

That alarm came so suddenly that Minter started forward with a leap and reached for the door of the inner room in which the safe was located; but the palm of his hand struck it with such force that it swung forward out of the tips of his fingers. Minter, realizing what he had done, reached again with a moan of anxiety, but although he caught the inner knob, the door had already closed with a soft click.

He twisted hard, but it had locked automatically, and on the inside surface of the door there was no keyhole! That key with which they had opened it so easily in coming in was useless now. They were penned in a cage of steel bars which ran from the floor to deep sockets of iron in the ceiling, and there they must wait the pleasure of the first man to enter the bank, unless they could give Little Samuel a signal and he could force the lock from the outside.

These observations were made with a single sweep of the flashlight, which El Cantor turned about them, first close to the floor and then on the ceiling.

Minter, in a panic, groaned aloud: "We're gone!"

"Steady!" said El Cantor in some contempt. "Little Samuel will break a way out for us without any trouble. In the meantime—"

Here was a voice called outside the front door of the building, called twice and again, impatiently. Then a key grated in the lock, and they heard the door open, accompanied by a sighing breath of wind which rattled the loose paper and sifted the greenbacks which lay on the floor in front of the open safe.

"Odd!" they heard a heavy voice saying. "Let's have a light here. Why haven't Michaels and Jewel answered us?"

"Mighty odd indeed," said a second man, as a switch snapped and the building was flooded with light. "This has a queer look. Have they been patronizing some moonshine still, d'you think?"

"Nonsense," retorted the other. "I know those men as well as I know myself. I doubt if a drop of liquor has ever passed their throats, except as medicine."

"Where are they, then? And what's the meaning of that chair overturned and that cigarette butt dropped on the floor?"

An exclamation replied to him.

"Mr. Gorman," said the second speaker, "I'm going to call in a little help here. This may need investigating."

Minter, crouched on the corner as if to escape the flare of light which beat down upon him, at this looked wildly up to his companion. And El Cantor, although

71

sweat was beaded on his forehead, made a gesture of mute reassurance while thought was visible on his face.

Standing motionless, with his eyes half closed, his agile thoughts twisted back and forth like a cornered rat seeking for a loophole of escape.

"Hold on one moment," said the voice of Gorman. "There's the door of the safe room fast locked. That looks as though no harm has been done."

The other replied in muffled tones: "Use your common sense, Gorman. Your watchmen don't answer when you call for them."

"What of that?" replied Gorman. "I tell you, if those men are crooked, I'm a fool. I would stake my reputation on them."

"Not crooked—I don't mean that. Perhaps they have been rendered incapable of answering."

There was a slight quiver of the floor, a mute testimony of the violence with which Mr. Gorman had started at this grim suggestion. He was unable to answer at once. Then he spoke with a heavy brusqueness, as if breathing out his own fear.

"Killed, you mean? And so easily, so quietly, that there hasn't been a sound to alarm the village? My dear friend, you do not know Michaels. Even supposing that Jewel might have been mastered, I tell you that nothing on earth could down Michaels before he had time to put in at least one shot. That man is a demon with a revolver—he thinks with it, you might say!"

"And the overturned chair and the cigarette butt?" urged the other, still in that same alarmed and alarming half-stifled tone.

"The porter was careless when he cleaned up, that's all."

"What, Mr. Gorman? So careless that he left a cigarette butt ground into the floor? And who smoked that cigarette?"

72

"Why, man, there are millions—"

"Not in this bank! No one has ever been allowed to smoke here except in your private office."

"Damnation, man!" roared Gorman suddenly. "Do you infer that my bank has been robbed? I tell you, in twenty years— But we'll have a look at the safe. Wait till I have my key to the door and—"

There was a musical jingling of metal; then Gorman's companion in a renewed warning.

"Mr. Gorman, you have a gun. I'd carry a gun in my hand before I entered that doorway, I tell you!"

"Take a look in, then!"

At this alarming suggestion, El Cantor, moving as a snake moves when it hunts, swift as a drawn whiplash and silently as an owl's wing, reached the door of the towering safe and pushed it shut. Then he glided back and sank to the floor at the base of the paneling which surrounded the safe room. Was that paneling high enough to keep the two inquisitors from looking over?

Apparently it was.

"Can't even see the floor of the room," said the second speaker.

"Well, well! I'll open the door, but this is damned nonsense, I tell you."

"Your gun, Gorman!"

"Very well, then. Here it is. That'll satisfy you, I hope."

"My own gun satisfies me more. Gorman, I can still smell the cigarette smoke in the air. We'll find trouble here before we leave the building, I promise you that!"

Chick Minter, in the meantime, his lips snarling back from his tobacco-yellowed teeth, made the blue-steel length of a revolver glide out of his pocket ready to cover the doorway; but a thin, strong hand slid out, caught the weapon, and wrenched it from his grasp.

It was a face turned green with suspicion that jerked around toward El Cantor. But the latter was calmly dumping the cartridges out of the weapon. He handed back the harmless husk of the empty gun. Then, taking his own revolver by the barrel, he made a significant gesture as if cautioning Minter to use the gun in no more deadly fashion than as a club.

He went further. He dropped his own gun into his clothes again, and crouched on the floor bare-handed, in a position very like that of a sprinter on his marks and ready for the race. A second thought pleased him still better, and as the key was heard to click home in the lock El Cantor slipped still nearer and put his shoulder to the door.

The lock turned—and instantly the full lunging weight of El Cantor tossed the heavy steel door wide. It caught the bulky form of Mr. Gorman before it and crashed him to the floor with a yell of astonishment.

But behind him stood his companion, revolver leveled, mouth agape as though the scream had just issued from his own throat, and his eyes two white disks of glistening terror. The gun boomed, but the bullet spatted harmlessly against the front of the safe.

As for El Cantor, he had flung himself straight forward without hesitation, driving close to the floor. And the man with the revolver sprawled heavily on the floor with a wheezing grunt as the wind was crushed from his lungs.

The speeding form of Chick Minter was already through the front door of the building before El Cantor was on his feet, but the latter was running only a scant half dozen paces behind him as they rounded the rear corner of the bank and found the frightened Samuel before them. They did not need to pause to explain. Inside the bank Gorman and his friend were making noise enough to have roused an army, and there were already responses.

The doors of a dozen houses in the neighborhood

74

were slamming. Twenty armed men would be at the bank in as many seconds. And the three fugitives dashed straight ahead for the clump of trees in which the horses had been tethered. The light feet of El Cantor might easily have put him in front past Chick Minter, but he fell voluntarily back beside the laboring form of Little Samuel.

For running was the exercise least congenial to the giant. He could walk as fast as a jogging horse and keep it up for miles on end, but to heave his solid bulk into a run was a desperate effort. He trod like an elephant in the rear.

So it was that Chick Minter reached the horses first, and bad luck was with him. The three animals, for the sake of speed in their release, had been tethered with the three pairs of long reins twisted together. Minter, in releasing his own mount, released the others also. His cursing haste made the spirited young bay gelding which had carried El Cantor rear and plunge back. He tore the reins easily from the hands of Minter, and, turning, shot across the open way from the town and its increasing hubbub. That example was instantly followed by the other pair.

It takes all of a man's skill to master even one plunging horse. With two animals lurching back in opposite directions, Minter was helpless. And before El Cantor, sprinting forward in mad haste, could reach him, the last pair had torn away and were racing off through the night, tossing their tails and neighing in the wild joy of their recovered freedom.

10

The crowd which was already milling around the bank needed a far less broad hint than the sound of those ringing neighs to bring them in the right direction. They came now in a rush, yelling encouragement to one another, with the thick, rich voice of Mr. Gorman in the distance panting out offers of rewards.

And the three, looking back through the clear starlight from behind the scant shelter of the trees, saw that charge approaching like a rush of infantry. They did not pause. El Cantor led their flight into the nearest hollow. But there, instead of running straight on through the night, he turned sharply to the right.

"In heaven's name!" cried Chick Minter. "Are you gonna run right back into town?"

"They'll have horses after you in five minutes," answered El Cantor briefly. "Do you want to stay in the open with horses behind you, Chick?"

Minter, at that thought, swung obediently into line with the others, and they fled silently, Minter himself rushing impatiently into the lead. He dropped in at the shoulder of El Cantor for a moment.

"Let Sam go!" gasped Chick. "The two of us can never get loose with that damned black anchor around our necks!"

"Save yourself," said the other calmly, "I'm with Sam in this."

Chick Minter leaped away with an oath, but after a moment he faltered and drew back to the other pair again, as though he still trusted more to the brains of

El Cantor to save him and Samuel both, than to the speed of his legs.

They were doubling, in fact, straight back for the town and they gained greatly by that simple maneuver, more than half concealed, as they were, by the hollow of the draw through which they were passing. Only one man, running wide and somewhat to the right of that solid body which had plunged out from the bank, saw the three shadows laboring back toward Loughbury.

He shouted a challenge; then he sent a bullet after them which was promptly answered by El Cantor with a snap shot over his shoulder—a shot which came so perilously close that the pursuer instantly dropped flat on his belly and from that position of advantage began to pump lead at the fugitives.

He did nothing but bring back the current of the townsmen in the right direction, however. And Little Samuel, hearing the bullets whistle about him, grew frantic with fear and redoubled his speed with a sort of hysterical power. For twenty steps he sprang away even from El Cantor, gasping as he ran: "Lord, save me! I ain't ready to die."

After that spurt, his speed was gone. Still he plunged ahead with strides that might have shook the solid earth beneath him, but every moment his wind was failing, and now it came in hoarsely whistling gasps. He rolled the whites of his eyes at El Cantor, and the latter replied with a reassuring gesture.

There was little assurance in his heart, however. For the leaders of the pursuit were gaining on them at every step. He tried another shot or two into the air, but not so high that the runners could not hear the whistle of the bullets. That had the salutary effect of making them draw back to the bulk of the townsmen. In this way they pressed ahead into the town, cleared the first row of houses, and ran straight down the main street.

They were spotted instantly. From the black shadow in front of one dwelling a man opened hasty fire from a revolver. But starlight is not conducive to accurate revolver play. His shots went wild and only spurred Little Samuel to a renewed burst of speed. It ended with the giant doubled far to the side, his face contorted as he gasped in his breath, his feet pounding crookedly into the dust.

The short grade of the railroad was a long hill to Little Samuel and when he reached the top he gasped to El Cantor "Go on—I'm done. Don't bother about me."

It was in fact the end for the big man, and El Cantor glanced wildly about him. Straight behind them came the pursuit, well bunched, two or three of the leaders pressing out away from the others, however, as they saw the game so nearly at a close.

A string of empty box cars stood on the siding near the station house. Toward them El Cantor led the way, but as he ran he saw a thing which gave him a first glimmer of hope—a hand car on a second siding, near the first, but backed up on a sharply sloping pair of rails with a block under the front wheels.

He needed only to swing his arm toward it. The others understood. By the time he had torn the block away, Little Samuel and Minter had swarmed onto the hand car. The steep grade gave the heavy truck the first precious impetus. A moment later, the tremendous heave of Little Samuel on the handles caught the car as a wave catches a small boat and shot it rattling across the junction with the main track.

At the same time the pursuit, topping the railroad grade in a mass, saw the fugitives heading down the track. The hand car was already lurching away faster than a man could run. Their legs could never overtake the prize, but their guns very well might, and in an

78

instant a fusillade was rattling. It combed the air around them. It whistled above; it thudded on the cinders beneath.

But it was only for a moment. Three men, and one a giant, were straining their hearts to give the hand car greater speed, and once started rolling, it gained smoothly; presently it was whirling along as though it were tied to an engine. And the firing ceased except for a moment or two, the long, metallic clang of a rifle firing down the track. Then they were alone with the rush of the wind against their faces.

After that, they relaxed their labors. Chick Minter, having been on the verge of despair, now passed to the other extreme. He still worked at the handle of the flying car with one hand; with the other he swung his hat in cowboy style and yelled like an Indian. Little Samuel, however, had turned devout. This strange deliverance worked powerfully upon his imagination.

"I'm gonna leave this here life," he told El Cantor. "They's a day comin' when even you, sir, ain't gonna be able to save me. And if they got a rope big enough to hold me, they's gonna hang me, sir! They's gonna send this poor soul to hell if they get a chance!"

El Cantor replied not a word to all of this. He sat on the edge of the truck with the wind whistling about him, sheltering his cigarette skillfully from the blast, and regarding the brightness of the stars with the bland eye of a child.

The railroad was bearing them closer to Gloryville with every mile they covered. Presently it would swing away to the right and at that point they must leave it. In the meantime, this was a pleasant incident and he enjoyed it to the utmost.

"Is there another town near on this road?" he asked Minter suddenly, as they passed from the broad plain into a valley heavily forested, with the rush of a stream somewhere in the black heart of it, or showing as a white curve here and again.

"I dunno," said Minter. "All I know is that I'm glad I'm here. Damn the towns. We could breeze through 'em fast enough."

"Bullets," said El Cantor coldly, "travel faster than a hand car. What's that light ahead?"

A growth of tall trees now bordered the railroad on either side, so that the rails themselves were twin streaks of uncertain light dipping straight through a rough chasm of darkness. And out of this blackness ahead, a faint ray of light struck.

"Most like, a camp fire," suggested Minter carelessly.

"Don't you ever study the lay of the land?" asked El Cantor, in the voice of one studying a problem in character.

"Why should I?" asked Minter. "I ain't a geographer."

"I'll give you one good reason," said El Cantor. "Because you don't know the country you work in, they'll take you and string you up, one of these days, Minter. That's a prophecy!"

He spoke with such an acid of contempt that Minter turned over in his mind an ugly answer and then decided that the risk was not worth the pleasure. In the meantime, a second light gleamed beside the first.

"Another camp fire, perhaps," suggested El Cantor sarcastically. "Slow up, Samuel. We may need to think this over!"

Sam accordingly decreased the speed with which he had been pumping the car along. They began to coast smoothly, slowing every moment, but as the sound of the clicking, rumbling wheels died away, they heard another growing murmur which swept up the track straight toward them.

"A train, doggone me!" cried Minter.

"No train," answered El Cantor. "A searching party."

80

"For what?"

"For us."

"Coming this way? Are you plumb turned around, partner?"

"You fool," snapped El Cantor, whose patience seemed about at an end, "can't they run circles around us, no matter how fast we go? Haven't they the telegraph to send out their warnings? Minter, I don't understand how you've lasted so long in your game!"

Minter gathered his sullen spirit for a reply equally caustic when all speech was cut short on his lips. Around the curve just before them, hurtling along on the down grade like a flying passenger express, with some dozen pairs of stout hands lending it power, came a hand car literally bulging with men.

There might be twenty, there might be thirty men in that jumbled mass which, at the distance, was impossible to count. But the dark clot of men was slashed with dim little lines of light, giving back the radiance of the stars.

"Rifles," said El Cantor. "Sam, we have to hoof it again!"

11

Half a dozen flash lights at the same time gleamed from the other ear, turning it into an indistinguishable mass of darkness, while a dim, broad focus of light fell upon the three fugitives. And what a yell of greeting rose for them! It rang and wailed through the night air with an inhuman exultation.

In the meantime the three had brought their own car to an abrupt stop, and they tumbled down to the ground with El Cantor leading the way and Minter protesting vigorously.

"We're getting into strange territory out here," he said. "Cut back the other way, if we got to go across country. You hear me, partner? You hear me? Head straight for Gloryville. We can lose 'em there!"

"Wait," said El Cantor, and ran on through the dark with Little Samuel following, and Minter, after two or three unhappy hesitations, finally surrendering to his fear of being left alone and to his belief in the superior brains of his companion.

The forest had closed thick around them when they heard the car of the posse stop. No hard thing to tell, for there was a crash that echoed miles away. They had not been able to check their flying impetus and had smashed into the empty car.

"Some broken necks, I hope," snarled Minter.

"You're wrong," said El Cantor. "That was not quite loud enough. That bump merely helped them to stop a little more quickly. And here they are after us!"

As he spoke, a shaft of light, half of it cut away by the shadow of a broad tree, shone through from behind and vaguely illumined the way. Other lights joined.

"They've got their sunshine along with 'em," groaned Little Samuel. "But if they ain't no runnin', I don't care how far we got to go."

It was a second growth forest, dotted here and again with some primitive giant—sometimes a mature tree, sometimes a glorious and tragic old stump thunder-riven and weather-worn, but still with a head lifted a hundred feet in air like a tower. But the second growth trees were closely wedged, and to fill the interstices between the trunks there was a dense growth of shrubbery and vines.

Those trailers and creepers caught at a man's feet and snared them like a lasso in expert hands. And the shrubbery had to be broken through by sheer strength.

It was folly to think of making one's way noiselessly through such impedimenta. Poor Minter, less muscular than his companions, clawed and struggled in vain. He could hardly make an impression on the jungle of greenery.

While El Cantor slid with an oily ease through the thicket, Minter had to fall back and wait behind the giant servant, taking advantage of the path which he beat open before him.

The noise they made was luckily covered, to a great degree, by the shouts and the crashings which announced the progress of the pursuit behind them. Then a wild clamor rose, followed by the cessation of all voices and a sudden drawing together of the lights.

They had found the trail and they were coming down it at a fair clip, while only the Herculean strength of Little Samuel in breaking trail enabled the three to maintain any lead. He was at work like a Titan. This was nothing that called for lightness of foot, and he fairly ripped the forest asunder and laughed with the joy of his might. Brush, even young saplings, he smashed down with his feet.

The almost impenetrable thicket he tore asunder with his great hands. And behind him, in a cloud of dust, with flying branches whipping their faces, came El Cantor and Minter like calves behind some monster bull, the king of the herd.

Even so, the others gained until Little Samuel broke out suddenly into an open stretch with the stars picking out the foam of the white water where the river swept around a sharp curve in its course down the valley.

"Take to the water!" ordered El Cantor, and led the

way down until the currents, striking him at the knees, cast spray as high as his waist.

"It ain't possible!" thundered the giant above the voice of the water. "We can't swim this here. We can't do it, sir!"

But here the leader turned abruptly up the stream, striving to run, and in the terrible grip of the water managing no more than a fast walk. For a few rods he kept on in this fashion until the lights of the posse, like a many-eyed dragon, drew closer and glared out at them from among the trees, threatening to break into the clear at any instant. Then he paused, and yelled to Little Samuel to carry them both up the bank.

It was nothing for the great black. He took one on either hip and went up the bank with his long strides, gained the more level going, and was instantly among the woods, while below them, with shouts, the posse poured into the open valley.

Where the thicket began once more, El Cantor and Minter dropped to the ground. Here, in the heat of the battle, so to speak, El Cantor ordered a halt, setting the example by throwing himself flat on his back.

Minter called it madness, but El Cantor explained. The posse most probably would follow downstream, when they found that the tracks entered the water. Then, finding no back track, while the river was still fordable, they would swing back up the bank once more. This must cost them priceless time, and meanwhile the three, with strength recruited by a rest, however brief, would be doubly prepared for giving them a hard chase.

That logic could not be denied. For three grim minutes, with hostile voices beating up and down the river, they lay there, breathing deep, letting the cool of the forest mold temper their fevered bodies. And when the lights of the posse turned back up the stream, El Cantor sat up.

A yell like the baying of hounds announced the discovery of the trail where it left the water. Then one strong voice took command and gave directions.

"One of 'em dropped out here. He turned yaller and quit the water the quickest. Them that had the nerve stuck by the water and got farther up the stream. They are the ones we want. Steve, take a couple of the boys —Charlie and Mack, you go along with Steve. Run down this here trail. The rest of you foller me. And foller me smart. You ain't done sweatin' this here night. Keep your guns ready. We ain't gonna waste no time askin' questions when we see something move."

After that, the mass of noise swept farther up the stream.

"Now?" said Minter in a whine of eagerness, rising to his feet.

"Stand fast," El Cantor commanded. "Let them listen to the silence for a while."

A moment later, as the noise of the posse grew dim in the distance and the voices of the river dominated the place once again, they heard three men approaching, and approaching slowly, slowly. Little Samuel started to his feet, breathing hard with fear; the hand of the master gripped him, and he was quiet again.

"Wait!" whispered El Cantor. "They have been with a crowd, and it has kept their spirits up. They're not in a crowd now. Let's see how they like this darkness."

They did not like it at all. Volleyed curses announced every step of their progress. The wild swerving of the one light which served them told how they were stumbling over roots and tangles of vines. Then they paused. They were not ten strides distant. Their voices were perfectly audible, even though they were not raised.

"Old-timers," said one, "this here gent, to judge by his sign that he leaves behind him, is a sort of a giant."

"I seen him clear as day when he hit into the trees,"

85

said another instantly. "About seven feet he was. Damned if I'd pick him out for a fight on this sort of a night. He could smash the three of us to bits before we could ever get our guns workin'. I'd rather foller a mountain lion into a cave than be trailing this here gent blind like this. Damned if he ain't lyin' low right now, waitin' for us to come along. Listen! They ain't a sound—not a damn sound! He's layin' for us, boys. What's three men to a gent like him?"

"Wait! There's something now!"

"Nope. Only a touch of wind off yonder."

The third said simply: "I'm sick of this here promenadin' by night. I got a day's work to do to-morrow."

The shamefulness of this confession of weakness was greeted with a moment of silence.

"Well, Steve," said the last speaker, "what're you aimin' for us to do?"

"Why," said Steve at last, "you could see that the old man didn't set no stock by this gent. Otherwise he wouldn't have give us three the job. He'd have sent a third of the boys along on the trail. I say, let's go back and have a smoke. Then we'll tell 'em that we lost the trail in the woods. Here, partner, drop that light and stave in the glass. We'll tell 'em that we busted our light. That's good enough for an excuse. Me, speakin' personal, I'm fagged some!"

At this, they turned slowly back, and when their voices had faded El Cantor rose, the others following, and once more they struggled into the forest. It was easier to break through in this line, however. The shrubbery was less dense, and Little Samuel pressed on like a steamroller with the others in his wake until they reached the line of the railroad. There they paused, and El Cantor lighted a match to see the time. After that he turned to Minter.

"Chick," said he, "you have a pocket full of money and a whole skin on your back. Go south, old son. Hit for Mexico. That five thousand will look like fifty south of the Rio."

"And you fellers?" asked Minter.

"Gloryville," said the leader.

"Gloryville? Ain't they apt to figger you out there?"

"It's a gamble. My job takes me there. So long, Chick."

"So long, boys."

He waited until they were far away, and then he spoke his rancor: "That there double cross! I ain't forgettin' it!"

But he received no answer, only the mumbled curse of the huge black man as he stumbled over a stone.

There was only one great goal before them now, and that was to reach Gloryville before full dawn. For if the first light of the day grew strong enough, there was no doubt that they would be seen by the early risers, and once seen and recognized, their clothes in tatters from the walk through the shrubbery, covered with dirt and with dust, it would be strange indeed if even the slow wits of Western justice did not waken and see in them the plunderers of the Loughbury Bank.

El Cantor pointed out this matter to Little Samuel, and tried to urge him to a run across country; but there was no run left in Little Samuel. All that he could do was to swing forward with a heel-and-toe walk which defied the efforts of any common man to keep up. The master had to break into a jog-trot time and again to stay with the big man.

The night turned cold, now that morning was not far away. And the wind, cutting sharply out of the north, chilled the scratched flesh and the bruised body of Little Samuel. His spirits ran very low, very low. He wrinkled his fleshy brow at the solemn face of the night, and the glistening stars shone on his rolling eyes.

"O Lord," moaned Little Samuel, "if I ever get my bones all stretched out warm and peaceful on a doggone

87

heap of hay ag'in they ain't nothin' gonna pry me loose! Not even you, sir!"

El Cantor chose to accept this remark with a jovial spirit, in order to raise the head of his big companion.

"That's what the cats say, Samuel," he answered, "after they're home in the morning with half an eye gone and the plume off the end of the tail. They sleep in a corner until noon, sun themselves in the afternoon, and lick their sore spots in the evening; but as soon as the night comes, Samuel, and puts masks on the houses they have been looking at all day, and turns the alleys into mysteries, they begin to smell the wind—and in a moment they are through the window, over the back fence, and out into the world again!"

Little Samuel sighed noisily.

"They ain't no place in life with you, sir," he anounced.

"Yes," said El Cantor. "Sometimes you'd like to sit on the wharf again with the heat of the sun between your shoulder blades and with the rod in your hands, and the line turning zigzag in the water with catfish somewhere in the shadows underneath. But, after all, you wouldn't trade that life for this. What?"

"What for is all this here ramblin' to me?" moaned Little Samuel. "You're smashin' banks and pilin' up riches and havin' your fun. But I don't see none of the money. They ain't no chance for me to set up by myself and start a home and get me a wife."

"Where would you be without me, Samuel?"

"I ain't picked out the exact place," admitted Samuel.

"I'll tell you," said El Cantor, a subtle change coming into his voice. "You lazy, shiftless, worthless, cruel devil, you'd be in jail, my friend, with a suit of stripes donated to you for nothing, and at night you'd sleep on a narrow cot, and every day you'd break rocks on the rock pile. D'you understand? Or perhaps you'd not be working.

"You'd only be waiting, Samuel, in a nice, roomy, airy

88

cell all by yourself, with two guards outside the bars all day and all night, with all the food you want and anything you could name—waiting, Samuel, until one bright day when you stood on a trap door with a rope knotted around your fat neck and a parson praying for your lost soul, my friend, and—"

"I ain't done nothin'!" cried Little Samuel in a burst of hysterical fear. "I ain't done nothin', and I ain't never gonna do nothin' that means hangin'!"

"You lie!" El Cantor declared coldly. "You love a knife and its ways and work too well, Samuel. You may keep away from it for a time, but in the end you'll go back to it. For instance, Sam, a dozen times you've fumbled the handle of your knife and wanted to slip the blade between my ribs—drive it home and twist it around in my heart. But something keeps you back. A little touch of fear—a very wise touch of fear, Samuel."

"I tell you, sir," cried Little Samuel, "that no idea like that ever—"

"Be quiet," answered El Cantor. "You have had the whip on your back to-night, and your spirit is rather low. But I know you, Sam. I know every treacherous thought that comes into that big head of yours. I know every thought that makes your fat fingers twitch. And when you lie to me, it makes no difference."

Little Samuel made no retort. But he put a little greater distance between him and his companion, and now and again, as they walked on, he glanced at El Cantor with flashing side looks bright with the bitterest hatred, bright with the most reverent fear.

In the meantime, their fast gait had swung them out of the valley across the steep ridges of two ranges of hills, down to the flat, where in the blackness the lights of Gloryville—dull and scattered lights at this hour—shone in the distance.

Then a gray line streaked the east, and grew, and

89

grew. The thin moon turned old, turned dull, and became no more than a wisp of cloud; voices began to sound in the houses of Gloryville; the beauty and the strangeness of the night left the mountains; and as the day came, Little Samuel and his master reached the hotel, and climbed through the back way—both with their boots off, working with silent, stockinged feet, and gained in this fashion their rooms.

Little Samuel had not spoken since he received the last stinging rebuke from his companion, but now he ventured on speech again.

"Where you gonna put all that you got out of the bank, sir?" he asked almost timidly. "Because if they come searchin' for us, they'll sure find that money, and then —heaven knows what they'll do to the two of us!"

El Cantor in the act of loosening his necktie paused, and answered: "There's not a great deal of money, Sam. Only about sixty-five thousand dollars."

Samuel stood up with eyes as bulging as if he were looking upon a murder.

"Sixty-five thousand dollars!" he softly breathed. "They'll hunt the world over, sir," he added. "We wouldn't be safe if we was to turn into woodchucks, and hide in a hole. They ain't no way of keepin' 'em from us. Where can you hide it?"

"Here," said El Cantor, opening a drawer in the small pine-wood table which stood in the center of the room. And in that drawer he deposited the packet with its rich contents. A second thought made him open the package.

Under the startled eyes of the black, he counted out the full amount—sixty-five thousand seven hundred and eighty dollars. Then he went on preparing for bed, but Little Samuel had lost all interest in sleep, exhausted though he was. He sat and stared at the table as if it were a cage containing a tiger.

In five minutes more the gray of the dawn was at the window, and El Cantor was sound asleep, but still the great black man had not stirred in his place. Fear, horrible and consuming fear, glistened in his eyes.

The passing voices in the street, the stir of the wakening people in the house, made him glance this way and that with a start of dread, but always his fascinated gaze came back to the center table, and hung upon it.

Then, as even these few moments wore away, he seemed to grow more accustomed to this stranger in the room, this lifeless presence more full of danger than a loaded gun. It took on another meaning, and his face was filled with thought.

He no longer stared at the table. Instead, he looked fixedly at his sleeping companion. Perfect rest was on the smooth brow of El Cantor. And in his sleep he smiled like a happy child lulled by an innocent dream.

Upon this, Little Samuel pored, and wondered. He could never understand this man, and because of that lack of understanding, his dread of El Cantor matched his hatred. Even now while the man slept, he feared him.

Yet it was not difficult to do, surely! He had only to take his knife from his belt, and steal across the floor of the room. One stroke, and the work was ended. One touch of his hand, and the drawer was open, the wealth within it was his!

And after that, long, endless days in the sun all his life—and bright raiment, and perfect ease, and some pretty girl with huge eyes and a flashing smile to help him spend the money.

He stood up slowly, leaning forward, resting his weight most gingerly upon his monstrous stockinged feet lest the floor should creak beneath him. For how less than nothing was needed to waken that sound sleeper yonder he knew too well! A breath, and bare thought was enough!

91

As a passing scent brings the wolf leaping to his feet, so the very shadow of danger might raise El Cantor!

Little Samuel paused in his stealthy progress, halfway across the floor, the sweat rolling down his face, although the morning was cold. Another step, and he could reach this sleeping devil.

At that instant the eyes of El Cantor opened wide, and looked forth upon the giant with the raised left hand stretched forth gropingly, and the rigid right arm at his side with something clutched tightly in the hand, so tight that the black skin turned to gray about the knuckles.

"Well, Sam," said he, "are you walking in your sleep?"

A blaze of ferocity shone for one moment in the eyes of the black man. So far as he knew, the white man had no weapon with him. His knife was in his trousers. His guns hung in their holsters on the wall, his rifle leaned in the corner of the room, a silent, gleaming witness.

Here the master was helpless, and if the knife were not used, perhaps a single grip of his great hands would break El Cantor's neck. Yet one could not tell. He would not dare to lie there so calmly if he were without resources. The ferocity sank away from Sam's eyes, died like smothered fire in his heart.

"I thought I heard something and I started for to—"

"To put your neck in that hangman's noose I was telling you about last night! Is that it?" said the other calmly, and so saying, he turned his back upon that ominous form, and drew a long, lazy breath of comfort.

But Little Samuel had heard enough, and too much. Here, certainly was no danger. With his back turned, how could El Cantor strike in his own defense?

Yet nothing under heaven, not the hope of salvation, could have persuaded Sam to move an inch nearer. The unknown thing stood over the sleeper, and guarded him; and before the brain of El Cantor, before the mystery, Little Samuel shrank back until he reached his own couch, and there he lay in a huddled heap, quaking until the floor shook with his mighty tremors at the thought of what he might have done!

12

Gloryville gave of its best men to form the posse which hunted for the three marauders who so mysteriously had given the slip to the posse, but the work which the hunters did was performed only half-heartedly. For the general opinion was that two of the three, and the money along with them, had been caught in the river, and washed to eternity while their bodies were broken up in the rush of the white waters.

There was some talk of running down the third man—the giant—but his stature was not generally believed. For it was pointed out by the doubters that all bandits are given a few inches gratis by those who describe them afterward; moreover, none of those who had seen this big man had been close enough to distinguish so much as the complexion of his skin.

Mr. Gorman published a statement, and offered a reward, and further stated that no depositors in the bank could possibly suffer. Rudy Michaels and Sam Jewel had been discharged summarily; the guardianship of the bank and its treasures would be placed in more competent hands thereafter.

Sheriff Walter Long, having sweated in vain for two days on the trail, decided that the matter was not decipherable. And he confessed as much to El Cantor who, on brilliant Monsieur le Duc, was the foremost of the riders who combed the countryside for the raiders.

"They ain't nothin' left to do," said he, "except to catch up that servant of yours, Little Samuel, and hold him. I figger that he's tall enough to fit the description of that one of the three that lined off by himself. And there ain't hardly nobody else in the countryside that would."

El Cantor smiled. "If I thought that the rascal had enough courage to try such a thing, I'd make him a partner."

"In the next bank you tackle?" grinned the sheriff.

"Exactly," said El Cantor, and grinned in turn.

That same night new mail of importance came to him by the skillful hands of Little Samuel. It was another letter from Margaret Swain to Hugh Nichols. It ran:

DEAR HUGH:

Since I received your telegram I can't tell you what a singing happiness has been in my heart. The weight is lifted, and I know that dad will win. I could never let you do such a thing if it were charity. But honestly I can't feel that it is anything more than a good business venture. Though I know that your own great heart is the only thing that has stirred you to do so much, and without any investigation of the property.

One thing troubles me a good deal—and that is how you may get safely to Gloryville with such a valuable thing as a certified check for sixty-five thousand dollars. I think, however, that I have solved the difficulty fairly well. You understand that I would be at the place with dad, but I want the whole thing to come as a beautiful surprise to him in the end. So I have arranged to have two of our most trusted men meet you at the Cranton station. That's the nearest railroad station to Gloryville, as you already have found out.

You will recognize the two men easily. One is named Francisco and one is José. Francisco has a bristly little mustache, and José rides a beautiful pinto, a perfect little fiend incarnate, but as fast as the wind and as durable as brass—and José loves it more than he loves life—next only to his love for my father.

If you wonder why I have sent Mexicans for such important work, I will explain. Cheap fiction has given a very black picture of Mexicans to some people, I know. But they are not all the same. Francisco and José were two peons practically enslaved on a great ranch in old Mexico when dad was there many years ago. He bought their liberty and then gave it to them.

Instead of taking the gift for nothing, they followed him all the way to the States, and they have never left him since that time. They are twin shadows. Wherever he goes, they go with him. And if they know that you are precious to my father, they will guard you like two second souls and good angels.

Besides, they are fine pistol shots, both of them, and they will use their guns at the slightest provocation. And in case of danger, that's the sort of man you must have with you. Not that there is to be any danger, because not a soul can know of the errand that is bringing you down here. However, I want to provide for the most impossible accidents, for if you do not arrive it will drive me mad!

I am so sorry that you cannot come until so close to the end of the time limit. But since you will be here the evening before the last day, that is enough.

It is more than enough, Hugh. I am not a religious person, as you know. But since that telegram I have gone back to my childhood and said my prayers at night—and put you in them!

95

Oh, Hugh, what a blessed thing it is to find one high-hearted man like you in the whole world!

PEGGY.

This last sentence claimed more of the attention of Señor El Cantor than all the rest. He read it thrice over, and then handed back the letter to Little Samuel in such a reverie that the giant took courage to peruse the contents hastily before he restored the letter to the envelope, and went about the delicate work of resealing. The dark brooding of El Cantor continued for some time. At length he rose, and flung himself on the bed.

He snapped an impatient finger. Little Samuel glided to him with cigarettes, and lighted the one he selected.

"The flies!" exclaimed El Cantor, and Little Samuel, picking up a big bamboo fan began to wave it skillfully above the head of his master with that peculiar weaving motion which produces the greatest current with the least whistling noise.

The fragrance of the Oriental tobacco filled the room. For an hour El Cantor lay moveless, then: "Enough!" said he, and sat up, while the weary arm of Little Samuel dropped heavily to his side. El Cantor kicked off his boots, slipped out of his trousers, jerked off shirt and belt.

"Do you hear, Samuel?" he said. "I am a young Spanish caballero, a young blood with time heavy on my hands, and nothing in my head but a girl's face. Quick!"

Little Samuel moved with the speed of one who knows his business. In a trice a riot of color appeared upon the bed. El Cantor made his selections by mute signals, and so, in five minutes more he was arrayed in a new splendor. He had on narrow trousers which flared wide about the ankles. He had on a rich yellow shirt—a golden yellow which flashed like gold leaf, and next he slid into

96

a tight-waisted Mexican jacket—overwoven with gold lace, and silver, like jewel work. Upon his head he placed the tall Mexican sombrero, that most romantic of head-gear which engraves the features in solemn shadowings.

Last of all, having spent some time on his scarf, which he arranged with the most precise care, he paused for a moment before the glass, with a vanity as frank as that of a woman, lifting his chin, turning his head, admiring the black brilliance of his eyes and the supple strength of his body as revealed by the close-fitting garments.

"Beer for your German," said he, "and ale for John Bull, and whisky for your hard-boiled Yankee, but for the dusky Mexican, the luxurious, time-scorning, imperious Mexican, wine, Samuel—only wine!"

With this mysterious remark, he knocked up one side of the brim of his sombrero to a rakish slant, took his guitar under his arm, and sallied forth. He went as usual down the back stairs of the hotel, circled around it with his soft step, and slipped across the street farther down. Then, by the garden wall which shielded the flowers, and the ladies of the house of Alvarez, he touched the strings, and sang:

> *Here in the silence and the dark hour,*
> *The petals are coldly furled,*
> *But open again, my dear, my flower,*
> *My blossom of all the world.*

There was a sound of a raised window, and the singer instantly struck with a will into the second stanza:

> *Oh, that my voice were the golden sun,*
> *For with a gentle art*
> *I'd touch the petals one by one*
> *And open wide your heart.*

97

And after that, sitting calmly on a stone on the farther side of the alley, El Cantor lighted a cigarette and waited patiently until his ear caught a sound fainter than that least whisper of a falling leaf in the autumn of the year. Then he leaped up, stamped out the cigarette and came close to the gate.

Behind that gate a tremulous, almost inaudible voice murmured: "Señor, señor, is it you? Señor Madman, is it you?"

"It is I," said El Cantor. "Therefore, open."

"Señor, in the name of mercy, leave us and—"

Here an angry whisper stopped her on the farther side of the wall. With that, there was the sound of a drawn bolt, and the door yielded the slightest inch. A shadow appeared at the crevice, but in that shadow El Cantor caught the gleam of an eye and the faint sheen of a red rose at the girl's breast. Instantly the hat left his head and he was on one knee.

"Alicia!" he whispered.

He heard her catch her breath. The door closed with haste, then opened waveringly again.

"Señor, rise."

"Alicia, I am too weak with joy—hearing you—seeing you!"

"Señor, I have come to end this folly, not to see you. I have come only to tell you"—here her voice fell to the faintest whisper—"never to come again to my father's house."

"The Blessed Virgin be praised!" moaned the duenna from the background. "This is the reward of my prayers to her."

"Hush!" said the girl, and stamped her foot.

And in the masking darkness, El Cantor smiled broadly.

"Ah," said he. "It is the unlucky song. It has displeased you, Alicia!"

"No, no!"

"Quickly, quickly my dear!" murmured the duenna.

"Stand far back, stupid!" cried the girl in a hushed voice of anger.

And El Cantor smiled broadly again.

"Again, señor," said the girl. "I beg you to go. I see you for the last time to say adieu."

"I have taught you to hate me?" sighed El Cantor.

"It is not that."

"Heaven be praised!" said he, and rose and stood above her, so that she shrank away and would have closed the gate, but his hand was upon it.

"My father's men—señor—"

"They will be blind."

"Señor, I beg you not to open the gate. It is a peril to my soul if you do."

Fear, perhaps, had so stolen her strength that she could not hold the gate with even the hand of a child, and it swung slowly open. He could see her more clearly—the gleam of the tall amber comb in her hair, and now more distinctly the dull red circle of the rose at her breast.

"My father!" murmured she, and beat her soft hands together.

El Cantor stepped through the gate and closed it behind him.

"Child, child!" cried the duenna in the distance, fluttering nearer. "You are mad to let him enter."

"He has come by force," sobbed the girl. "Now, señor, if they rush upon you, I shall see you torn to pieces."

"Tell me, Alicia, would it give you one moment of sorrow?"

"I dare not tell you."

"It is true, then. You would feel one touch of pity for poor Juan."

"Is that your name? I have never known it, really, though you have called me so freely by mine."

"Shall I call you señorita—and Alvarez? No, no, for there is only one name full of soft music, full of rare sweetness that fits you, my dear, and that is why I have called you Alicia, unpermitted. Do you forgive me now?"

"I forgive you. Hark! What is that?"

"That sound?"

"Yes! It was a footfall near us—I know not where!"

"My guardian angel, I shall show him to you!"

With a quick movement he caught the gate and jerked it open. There was revealed the enormous form of Little Samuel. So sudden had been the opening of the gate, so without warning, that he lacked the time to leap to the side. He was caught flatfooted.

"You see him," added El Cantor aloud. "My guardian angel is here."

He added under his breath: "You black dog, how have you dared to follow me?"

Little Samuel was struck with panic.

"It ain't spyin'," he stammered. "But I follered to help if they was trouble—"

"You lie," said the other. "But now stand in the shadow of that tree on the other side of the lane and wait for me. Come if I whistle."

He shut the door in the face of Little Samuel and turned again to the girl. She had run back to the side of the old woman at the apparition of the giant. El Cantor followed her and heard the duenna murmuring: "Go back to the house. If you love the safety of your soul, go back at once. Why do you stay? Why do you stay?"

"Old witch," said El Cantor sternly. "Leave us. Go back by yourself. I shall remain here with your mistress."

"Alone?" cried the duenna. "Heaven forbid!"

"You do not know me," declared El Cantor, "or you would not stay here to question me. Now, if you love the safety of that wrinkled hide that covers you, go back. And if you so much as whisper—"

100

So grim was the voice in which he spoke that the duenna lost the last shred of her courage and fled for safety. But when Alicia turned to follow her, she found El Cantor bowing before her.

What a picture as she shrank from him with her hands clasped at her breast and her eyes starry with fear!

"Señor, you will keep me here by force?"

"By just so much force, Alicia, as will set your conscience free. You have done nobly by that conscience. You have forbidden me to pass the gate, and I have entered by force. You have striven to retire to the house and I have stopped you—by force! And now, my dear, having done all that you could to retreat, you are free to stay here with me, and love me, Alicia!"

"Señor!"

"There is no other way. You must either hate me or love me."

The fear of Alicia seemed to have given way strangely to anger.

"Then I hate you, señor."

"Do you, truly?"

Oh, brazen and bold! He took one slender wrist; he drew her close to him.

"If you hate me, Alicia, there is only one way left, and that is to force you to care for me."

"Alas," cried the girl, "if my father were young, if I had a brother, you would not dare—"

"Tush!" said her. "This is very brave. I love to feel you struggle. You have such soft hands, my dear. They strike like the beating of wings of a moth. So—so! Now you are quite—very tired. Already so tired? No, Alicia, if you really hated me, hatred would have given you a greater strength, I swear. You observe, my beautiful one, that heaven must have intended you for me, or otherwise you would never have been so fashioned that your head would come to rest so neatly here in the

101

hollow of my shoulder at just a convenient distance for me to stoop and touch those delightful, panting lips!"

She burst into tears.

"You are making a mock of me!" she sobbed.

"I? A mock of you? Sweet Alicia, if you wish to teach me to love you more and more and more and more, you have only to fly into a passion and swear that you hate me. Will you swear it now?"

She lay in his arms, holding him close, her face pressed against his breast.

"I never meant it, Juan," she whispered. "I never truly meant it!"

"Dearest Alicia! Did I not know it? Could I not hear your heart speaking in spite of your words? In your voice, child, not the words you made it say. But a bird cannot change its song, and love has only one sound. As I loved you, I knew, surely, that you would love me. And so I came very rudely to hear you say it."

"Oh, Juan, it is a rough, rough way to woo a girl when you know already."

"But did I know? Was I right?"

"You are a demon! You have made me tell you!"

"Not I! I must have the words one by one, spoken by you. I must hear them come from your own throat, I must hear my name tremble out of it, once if never again. Tell me, Alicia."

"I am ashamed."

"Tush! You must tell me so. Raise your head."

"Do not make me, Juan. I shall die of it!"

"Now, sweetheart, look fairly up to me, my starry-eyed beauty! How sad it makes you to love me! But tell me that!"

"Let me hide my face again and I can tell you anything."

"No, in this way. Tell me: Do you love me, my rose of the world?"

102

Her lips parted, trembling, and her voice was a moan, and the fluttering of her heart beat warm and close to him.

"I love you, Juan. How dear you are to me. I have played at hating you. It was only so that I could taste my love for you more. My brave Juan, my beautiful, my glorious, from the first day I have worshiped you. Oh, my heart, it will break for joy, I must sing, but there is no song to say it!"

The voice of the duenna quavered: "There is some one coming! You are lost, child!"

"Old raven—old bad luck croaker!" cried Alicia Alvarez. "I am saved. I am not lost. See, Juan, there is no shame in me now. I want all the world to know what a glory has come to me. I want them to see me give myself into your hands, all of me—all my heart—all my body —all my soul. I want only one thing, and that is to know how I can make you happy!"

"Could I be happier than I am now? Could a man dream of more happiness?"

"Ah, yes. Even by the starlight I can see that there is a shadow in your eyes."

"Alas, Alicia, there is only one thing which troubles me, but that is a thing so great that not even you could help me with your love except to make me forget it."

"What is it? You cannot tell what I can do. Tell me, Juan!"

"It is a very strange story. I can only tell you that I must have by to-morrow two brave Mexicans—one with a short mustache, my dear, one with a pinto—a beautiful little pinto which he rides. Do you understand?"

"You must have two men—one with a pinto—it is like a strange fairy tale! Why must you have them?"

"For a very strange work. I have enemies, Alicia. You could never guess how many!"

"Ah," cried the girl. "Have I not seen you come like

103

a lightning flash and strike men down? Is it not for that that I love you? If you had not a friend in all the world, I should love you all the more. Hush, now. I must think. There is a thing in my mind. If I dare—if I dare—"

She drew a little back from him and struck her hands together.

"You will laugh, Juan. For it is a great jest! But listen—other men have told me that they love me; but not one of them dared to come like a lion, as you have come, and tell me so. Not one of them dared take me, as you have taken. They were sheep to me—sheep— sheep!"

She snapped her fingers.

"If they saw you, they could not help loving," said El Cantor. "A thousand eyes see the rose—only one hand can pluck it."

"Of them all," said she, "there are two brave men. Very brave. They would catch eagles and hunt lions for my sake. Why should they not hunt for you, also? As for the pinto horse, that I can manage also. My father has one.

"I shall have Luis ask for it. My father wishes greatly that I should marry him. He will give the pinto—I shall give Luis and Mateo to you to do what you choose with them.

"Mateo is very young. But he loves me very greatly. For the sake of me, he would have himself appear older. For my sake, therefore, he had grown a mustache. It is a thing to laugh at. And I have laughed, but he does not know at what. Therefore, he still loves me. Where shall they come to you?"

"Can you do this great thing for me, Alicia?"

"It is nothing. They would die for me."

"It is not to-morrow, then. But ten days from this I must have them. They must come to me at dawn by the three cypresses which stand together on the bank of the

104

river two miles above the town. At dawn, Alicia. Before the first red has come in the sky. They must be there. Can you promise them to me?"

"By my life I can promise them!"

"Why, Alicia, you are an enchantress. There is more power in those soft little hands of yours than in ten men. Ten men could not do so much for me."

"And you are happy now?"

"Happier than a king."

"Then I am happy, too!"

And she held up both her hands as if she offered her soul to him. The rose at her breast, crushed and drooping long ago, was dislodged by the gesture and fell unregarded to the ground.

13

Now in the dawn of the tenth day two horses pranced out from Gloryville, pressing hard on their bits, with the glory of the coming morning in their eyes, and the hunger for racing in their trembling legs. They reached the first great bend of the river, where it sways like an express train round a down-grade curve, and in the hollow arm of that curve they saw three great cypresses, three great sabinas planted fifteen score of years before, some said, by the Spaniards who had first founded a town in that region. It was the old predecessor of Gloryville.

It lived a century, died, was washed away by the fire and rage of an Indian victory, had its last remnants stamped flat by time, and now of the whole flourishing little town there remained for this distant generation only the three cypresses, monstrous past belief, great pyramids of greenery pointing heads forever tender, new, and sharp against the gray of the morning sky. And as the two riders came near to the cypresses, a third horseman started forth to meet them.

"It is El Cantor!" cried the rider who wore a feeble young mustache. "If Alicia needs help, how in the name of all the saints did she persuade that devil of a gringo to work for her? Can you answer that, Luis?"

"I cannot," Luis, replied gloomily, reining in the beautiful little pinto which he bestrode. "Unless," he added, "this work is not her work at all, but the service of this demon, this man-killer, this El Cantor himself!"

"Ten thousand fiends!" cried the first rider. "The same thought came that moment into my brain. He has won her; she has loaned him tools, and yet, Luis, what if we should be wrong?"

"Aye," nodded Luis, "What if we should be wrong? She is as proud as an angel, and if we failed her in this first service she has asked, she would lift her head and forget us forever."

"It is true!" sighed Mateo. "We must use our wits. And when this game seems to be his and not hers, we leave him in the lurch!"

Thus agreed, they made to the man on the red horse. He had halted and greeted them with a raised hand.

"One of you," said El Cantor, "is Don Mateo, and one Don Luis."

They acknowledged their names in turn.

"Señores," El Cantor added, "I presume you are familiar with the work which lies before us?"

The Mexicans glanced swiftly and darkly at each other.

"I am not," Don Mateo replied, "neither is my friend, Don Luis."

106

"Ah?" said El Cantor, and he raised his brows. "But I understand how this thing is. She was ashamed to confess what she wished to those who served her for love, and she left it to him who was hired for money."

"Money?" Mateo inquired.

"Money?" echoed Don Luis, with a lift of his fine young head.

"Certainly," said the man of sin, and he smiled blandly upon them. "She is a pretty thing. I admire her to the tips of my fingers. However, when one has a profession, one must stick to it. And I cannot afford to ride for the pleasure of riding and making ladies smile. And she knew it. She is an exceedingly clever girl.

"She said to me: 'Señor in this great matter there are only three men whom I can turn to. Two will serve me for kindness. You, señor, will serve me for money. You have only to name your price!' "

"And that?" asked Mateo, biting his lip to keep it from curling with scorn.

"A thousand dollars. A thousand silver pesos for a single day's work. This is not a bad stroke of business, you will admit. However, for a master workman, one must pay a master price!"

With this he tossed back his head laughing. Mateo stared upon Luis, and Luis upon Mateo.

"All is well," mentally said Mateo, stroking his young mustache.

"All is well," Luis likewise agreed. "The hireling is in her service, not his own. We may work with him heartily."

"As for the work," said El Cantor, "I shall describe it to you as well as I can while we ride along, but already we are close on our time for the first bit of it."

They struck off at a gentle dogtrot, the hoofs pattering like softly clapped hands of children. The first pink was in the eastern sky.

"From the house of Señor Swain, a little earlier than this," said El Cantor, "two men are riding for the station in the town of Cranton. In the first place, those two men must be stopped. Do you understand me, amigos?"

"Killed?" Mateo demanded a little huskily, with his eyes widening. "*Madre de Dios*, what a sin has Alicia drawn upon herself!"

"Killed, perhaps. But at least they must be stopped. When that work is ended, Mateo and Don Luis ride for Cranton, taking upon themselves the names of the men whom we have stopped—that is to say, you, Don Luis, are José. You, Don Mateo, are Francisco. In the old years, you were peons in Mexico."

"Ha!" cried the proud pair in a breath. "Peons?"

"It is the devil, is it not? I told Alicia that she could never find proud Mexicans who would take on such rôles even for her sake!"

"We are peons, then," growled Don Luis. "What next?"

"From your servitude in Mexico, Señor Swain bought you and gave you freedom. Out of gratitude, you followed him to this country and have remained in his service ever since."

"Service?" cried Don Mateo, instinctively gripping the butt of his revolver. "Damnation!"

"This happened years ago, when you were boys. You understand me? You are silent, fighting men. You speak little. Your looks are sour—as they are now, for instance. The train comes in—the long express. From the train there dismounts a man who recognizes you, Luis, by the pinto you ride—"

"Oh, cunning witch of a girl!" cried Luis. "For that reason I was given the horse!"

"You, Don Mateo, are known to be Francisco by your mustache. The man calls you by name and asks if you are to be his guides and his guards to the ranch of Señor Swain. You confess that you are. You mount him upon a third horse—"

"Where is that to be secured?"

"I shall present that horse to you presently. You ride out on the road toward the Swain ranch. You soon leave the road and cut straight across country. Presently you take an opportunity. You clap a gun to the head of the señor, whose name is Don Hugh Nichols. You tie him hand and foot. You leave him lying in the road. That is all!

"This work done, you ride on, you return to Gloryville, you receive the tears and the thanks of Alicia, and then you make a little journey to your estates in old Mexico until the dust and the trouble which this affair may raise shall have settled. As for your faces, they can never be traced, for Don Hugh will never see them again!"

This tale, simple as it was, left the youths sweating with anxiety.

"I observed to the señorita," went on El Cantor smoothly, "that this was dangerous work. She swore that she knew two men to whom danger was as a mouse to a lion. They regarded it not!"

A word of praise is sometimes as strong as the sword of the conqueror. It brought blood now to the faces and to the hearts of the two.

"All of this is very clear," said Don Luis, "but it seems to me that the lion's share of the danger and of the trouble comes to us. What of you?"

"For my work," El Cantor replied, "I am to receive only hard cash."

It was a retort of a nature that silenced them both; and so all three rode on in a dead quiet until they came to a high pitch of the road with tall pines over them, and at their feet a sharp decline into a narrow little valley through which a trail wound, weaving swiftly among the boulders.

The horses grew quiet, their panting ceased, they began to lift their heads and look about them with a gentle curiosity. They hearkened to the squirrels which chattered among the farther trees—then boldly just above their heads. They heard the whispers and the hushings of the wind. They breathed of the purity of the pines which filled the air. And so did their riders.

"Rein back your horses behind the trees, señores," El Cantor directed. "We have spent longer upon the road than we should have done, I fear. Rein back and let nothing of you be seen from below."

He spoke quietly, as one used to command, and they obeyed him without a murmur. For the thrill of the adventure was beginning to settle upon them. And they had hardly taken new places when they saw the reason for these precautions. A thin dust cloud blew down the heart of the little valley. The dust dissolved and became only a thick veil through which they could see two horsemen and a led horse, saddled and bridled.

"You observe," said El Cantor calmly, "that our two men are approaching and a led horse is with them. On that horse Señor Swain is to ride. It is my duty to secure it. For the moment, adios, amigos!"

As he spoke he took out a mask of thinnest black silk which he settled over his face leisurely, then drew on his hat, heavy and brilliant with its metal trappings. And after that, as a falcon stoops out of the sky, so swept the red bay horse down the declivity.

Like a bird indeed, swerving among the trees at an incredible speed, he rushed his rider down into the valley, but all so smoothly that they started no noisy little avalanche of rocks behind them. And the two horsemen proceeded straight on up the valley, unattracted by the slightest noise.

In the meantime, El Cantor was lost to view. The two riders came nearer. They were almost directly beneath the two on the hill.

"By heaven!" exclaimed Mateo suddenly. "I see through the design of the villain. He intends to wait until they have passed him a little, and then he will pistol them from behind!"

"It is that!" breathed Don Luis. "Mateo, we are damned if we stand by while such a thing is being done. Let us shout a warning—"

"Hush!" gasped Mateo. "What does he mean?"

He pointed with a stiff arm. In the heart of the valley through a gap in the trees they could see the strangers come to an abrupt halt before the form of a man who had leaped suddenly out before them—a masked man with a revolver in either hand.

Metal flashed into the fingers of the attacked pair; from the muzzle of one of their revolvers thin smoke spurted, and smoke, too, curled up from the guns of El Cantor. Then he who rode upon the right was struck from his saddle to the ground. The second bowed far over in the saddle.

And after all this, three chattering reports of guns came up to the ears of Mateo and Luis followed by the crowding echoes, indistinguishably mixed.

"A miracle!" breathed Don Luis. "He has killed them both."

"Heaven save me from him," answered Mateo. "Where are they now?"

For the picture had disappeared from the gap among the trees.

"He has taken them away to lie and rot under the pines. What a fiend—what a fiend!"

111

The tardy minutes slowly passed. A blue jay began to scream among the topmast twigs of a pine tree. And then they saw El Cantor coming again, with three horses led behind him.

"It is true," breathed Don Mateo. "The murderer has led away their horses. He will sell them to increase his thousand dollars. No doubt he has been through their pockets. A thrifty devil! I have only one wish—that heaven would give me courage enough to stand up to him and strength enough to stamp out his life!"

"Amen," said Don Luis solemnly.

The conquror came up to them. Not a fold of the rich bandanna about his throat was disarranged. He was as smooth and as smiling as if he had ridden down into the valley to shoot a squirrel for supper.

"I have had to bring three horses instead of one," said he, "to keep them from following!"

"To keep them from following!" cried Don Mateo. "Do ghosts ride horses, señor? Do they need saddles and spurs?"

"Ghosts?" inquired El Cantor. "Do you imagine that I have killed them? Don Mateo, Don Mateo! What manner of bungler do you think I am? No, I have spent all this time binding up a wound in the shoulder of the brave Francisco. He damned me through his teeth every moment I worked.

"Don José, however, was nicked in both the shoulder and the head. The infernal bullet glanced up from the shoulder bone and touched the side of his head. I was worried for a moment when he dropped to the ground. However, he turned out to be less hurt than Francisco, and both of them are well enough and have will enough, if we permitted, to jump into a saddle and ride for Cranton ahead of us. We must take these horses along, and turn them loose a little later."

"I thank heaven," declared Don Mateo. "A moment

112

ago," he added, "I was cursing you for a murderer!"

At this El Cantor favored him with a glance as sharp as the prick of a knife point. But there was no anger in his voice. "You are an honest man, señor," said he. And he continued: "There was a time when I aspired to the same dignity, but I am indolent by nature, and therefore I gave up the work for this—" And he waved down to the heart of the valley.

It was a hushed and respectful pair that followed him into the lowlands again and saw him turn loose the captured pair of saddle horses among the smaller hills. Only the led horse he retained, a stalwart brown gelding which was the favorite of Henry Swain himself. Another mile or so he continued in their company. Then he drew rein and passed the lead rope to Don Mateo.

"In this place," he said, "you will stop Señor Nichols, dismount him, and tie him hand and foot. Then you will leave him lying in the trail and ride on. You understand, my friends?"

They nodded, after which he raised his hat to them as gallantly as any Mexican gentleman, and they rode off side by side. They did not speak for some time; then it was Don Luis who announced: "I would not have him for my enemy, Mateo."

Mateo shuddered.

"You are a wise man, Luis," said he. "And now that I know his price, I shall never rate any difficulty higher than a thousand pesos. But, Luis, what can be the purpose of Alicia? What under heaven can she gain from all this? And what will happen to this Señor Nichols after we leave him tied hand and foot?"

"If he is to fall into the hands of El Cantor," Luis replied, "at least we know that he will not be murdered. As for Alicia, she is beautiful enough to have fallen into all sorts of trouble. I do not care even to think your question!"

They were half an hour in Cranton before the train came thundering to the station. But by that time their horses at the hitching rack had been breathed and were dancing again—particularly the tall brown, which had not carried a man's weight on the journey out.

Several passengers alighted from the train, among them a big young man with a clean-cut, fighting jaw, and smiling, steady gray eyes. He swept the surroundings from the station platform. Then he headed straight for Luis on the pinto. When he was near, he stopped short as if in surprise, then went on more slowly.

"You are Henry Swain's man?" he asked.

Luis nodded.

"I thought," said Hugh Nichols, "that you would rather be older by ten years, at least. However—this is your companion—this man with the mustache? Very well. It is clear enough. I am Hugh Nichols. You are to show me the way to the Swain ranch, I believe?"

In another minute he was mounted. He had donned riding clothes for that ride and the rest of his outfit was held in a fat-sided case of flexible leather which was easily strapped on behind the saddle. He rode well, moreover.

Although he was accustomed to an English saddle, a horse is a horse, and he adjusted himself readily enough. Once or twice he attempted to ask questions, but he was received with inaudible grunts, for both Luis and Mateo were doing their best to live up to the characters which El Cantor had told them that they must assume.

Their surliness had accomplished another and more unpleasant result, however. When they reached the appointed place, and Don Luis suddenly presented his revolver at the head of the victim, the muscular right arm of Hugh Nichols snapped forth as if he had been prepared for just such an attempt.

114

His fist caught poor Luis an inch to the right of the point of his chin, drove back his head like the impact of a cannon ball, and knocked him clean from the saddle. When he turned on Don Mateo, however, he found himself confronted by a gun held in a steady hand, and a grim face behind it.

"If you stir," said Don Mateo, "I fire, señor. You are a very brave man. I hope that you are not a very foolish one also. For I promise you, señor, that the instant you move, I shoot you through the heart. Luis, stand up and tie his hands from behind!"

It was done. A man knows when it is folly to resist. But while he was forced to dismount, while he was bound hand and foot, Hugh Nichols groaned forth his rage and shame.

"I should have known," said he. "By heaven, I *did* know when I first laid eyes on you!"

"Señor," said Mateo suddenly unable to resist temptation, "I can tell you one thing only. No harm is to come to you at our hands."

"Harm?" shouted Nichols. "Damnation, man, in stopping me in the midst of this ride you have done me more harm than if you had chopped off a leg."

He added: "But I know there will be no murder. Murder does not fit with a face like yours. There is too much honesty in your eyes. But, Francisco, or whatever your name may be, go one step further as an honest man should do.

"Whoever persuaded or hired you for this work, persuaded you with lies or hired you for not a tenth of what I would pay to be free. Consider this, Francisco—I am a rich man, you may name your price. It shall be yours on my honor, and my honor has never been broken. Do you hear me?"

A faint smile touched the lips of Mateo.

"Señor," said he, "I am sorry for you. But we have done our work. Señor, adios! I hope that help comes to you before the evening grows dark, and the lobos come out."

So they left Nichols sitting in the path and rode away. After that he spent a busy half hour working at the bonds. But they were too securely fastened. He ended in a sweat of rage and grief when, lifting his head to draw a longer breath of the warm air, he heard a noise that was sweetest music to his soul.

Far off he distinguished a light jingling of bells—it drew closer, it was a rhythmic shower of ringing, like that which is made by the bells on the horses which draw a sleigh. This, however, was a far lighter and more delicate sound, and every bell, although small, had a voice of its own, a tone higher or deeper, so that they chattered in a sweet, everchanging chorus.

Then he made out two men against the first red of the sunset, for the sun had just dropped below the horizon. They came on swiftly toward him. He managed to stand on his feet, although he maintained a precarious balance there, so tightly were his legs bound together.

He shouted. He must not risk failing to call their attention. For there was still ample time. He had until tomorrow. And if need were, and he could learn the right direction, he could push ahead on foot and make the goal of his journey.

They were nearer. They were immediately above him on a little swell of the ground. He could see them clearly, now—one a gigantic fellow, walking, one a man mounted on the noblest horse that Hugh Nichols had ever seen; and the faces of both were masked.

At that his heart failed him. The giant strode toward him.

"My friend," said Hugh Nichols, "if you are not a party to this plot—if you are merely out on the road to—"

116

"Stranger," the big man interrupted in a voice as thick and as huge as his physical bulk, "they aint no use talkin'. Jest you rest easy, partner. They ain't gonna be no harm done to you!"

So saying, with a hand as resistless as a steel talon, he deposited Hugh Nichols on the ground, and began a methodical search of his clothes. Every pocket was turned out. His watch, his cigarettes, some old business letters in his coat, his wallet were taken one by one and placed upon the great silk bandanna of the giant, spread for that purpose beside the road.

The loot at length was gathered together, the ends of the bandanna drawn up, and the monster carried the booty back to the rider who remained at a little distance. Hugh Nichols strained his eyes eagerly toward the latter, but there were many yards between them, and moreover, against the horizon, the horse lost color and appeared a black silhouette. Only the distinguished beauty of its form was apparent. He could tell that and he could tell, also, that the stranger was of ordinary stature. All the rest was vague.

But now he saw the rider, after rapidly sifting through the booty in the bandanna, select a single envelope, which he tore open, examined for a moment, and then lighted a match and set it on fire, waiting until it burned to a black cinder that floated away on the light breeze.

Nichols at last understood, and his heart burned with a futile rage, a futile despair. By some mysterious foreknowledge the purpose of his coming had been discovered, and he himself had been trapped, and the salvation of Henry Swain was impossible—the winning of the girl must be fought out again from the start!

14

Señor El Cantor, having burned that certified check and the envelope which contained it, having stripped from poor Henry Swain his last defense, having stolen the work of his daughter from the very tips of her reaching fingers, smiled to himself like a man who has just completed a really good and great action.

He watched the light cinder blow away, saw it dissolved in a fine black dust in the desert wind; then he loosed the rein of Monseiur le Duc and spoke to the stallion. Off they shot at that tireless gallop with which the red bay made play with the miles. And as he rode, El Cantor lifted his head and sang songs with formless words and piercing notes.

He had conquered.

He swung far out from the straight course to Gloryville and aimed at the house of Henry Swain in the hope of a moment's glimpse, a moment's word with Margaret. Fortune favored him again.

Before him, through the dull twilight, an obscure dust cloud arose. He swept upon it at that swinging gallop, tireless and easy, until it dissolved into a rider, and this to a woman's figure, and last of all, he knew the exquisite grace of Peggy herself, with her head canted a little to one side. How earnestly she rode, keeping her horse stiffly in hand! And something told El Cantor that she was striving to flee from some inward anguish of the spirit.

She did not turn her head until he drew up beside her.

Then what a cry of anger and of pain came from her lips. Even Señor Jingle Bells winced a little, and his matchless poise deserted him for the least instant.

"It is you, John Albert!"

"It is I," he answered. "Is there trouble?"

"It was you," the girl charged fiercely. "You met Francisco and poor José. You shot them down. Oh, I know it as well as if I were there and had been able to look through your mask at your hateful, smiling face!"

Jingle Bells grew a little pale, but it was only the weakness of a moment. He recovered his nonchalance almost at once.

"I observe," said he, "that I am often in your thoughts. What is this?"

"You will deny it!" she cried. "But denials make no difference to me. I've seen the truth. I know the truth!"

"Of what, Peggy?"

At this familiar nickname coming from him, she drew a sharp breath of outraged dignity. But how could she argue such a point with such a man? She merely let him see the glitter of her eyes and the gleam of her teth as her lips parted.

"Of the shooting of Francisco and José," said she.

"Tush! Are they dead?"

"You very well know that they are not. And it was you who stopped them. It was you who shot them down!"

"Really?" said Jingle Bells, smiling upon her again. "This would need proving, you know. It is foolish to talk of murder until one can talk of hanging also."

"I have no proof," she admitted. "You were too clever to leave any behind you. And that's like you, John Albert. You commit no crime except safe ones. There is not even courage in you. Do you hear me? You are a coward—a coward!"

She had drawn her horse to a stop. It was dripping

119

with sweat, and had been so hard-ridden that it dropped its head and made no offer to move on the way home. What a passion had been in the rider! What a passion was in her still!

John Albert listened, and instead of making a reply he took an easy position in his saddle and lighted a cigarette. He was watching her as one would watch a painting, impersonally. There was a strength in the silence that made Margaret Swain bitterly regret the tirade which had just burst from her lips. It was unladylike—it was childish. But there was such a torment of grief and rage in her heart that dignity went down before it.

"I didn't know that you could be like this," said John Albert. "I like you better this way. With those blue eyes and that pale gold hair, I was almost afraid that there was not enough blood in you. I see that there's plenty of that. Plenty!"

He added: "But the proofs being lacking, you know, and nothing but guesswork left—"

"It is not guesswork. There is no one man in the world who could beat both those men at once—no one in the world except you!"

"Peggy, this is unexpectedly flattering."

She thought then, as she looked at his beautiful dark face and the quiet smile on it, that God could not have devised in human shape a more hateful thing.

Then the last burst of pride made her cry: "But it's all useless, John Albert. He doesn't need a guide to reach me. Whatever deviltry taught you that he was coming, it didn't teach you that he's a *man!* And he'll not need a guide to come to me. He'll walk the distance.

"Nothing will stop him—nothing! Not ten men like you with all your tricks. And in the end, John Albert, in the end he'll smash you under his heel until you whine for mercy—until you beg!"

"Dear Peggy," said El Cantor, "I am so sorry that you

120

care so much for him. He's an extraordinarily fine fellow at that."

All the color dropped from her face.

"You've met him then?" she whispered.

He answered indirectly: "I have brought the money to you, Peggy. Here in this wallet is the full sixty-five thousand dollars. I didn't intend to give it to you until the last day—until to-morrow, of course.

"But now something tells me that you will not be able to get the help you need before you can pay back this money. You will only have to do a very beautiful thing—buy that Solway place and give the deeds to your father before sunset.

"He will be the happiest man in the world, I presume, and the most curious. While he is in that happy mood, I suppose that you'll tell him you owe his deliverance to the man who is about to become your husband?"

A half dozen times she had been on the verge of interrupting him, but his unhurrying voice went on, and every word he spoke brought the realization more coldly home to her—that this was the only way! And at last she merely took the proffered wallet in both her hands and her head dropped weakly, surrendering.

"Will you tell me one thing?" she asked.

"Questions are usually embarrassing. But I'll try, of course."

"Is Hugh Nichols alive?"

"Hugh Nichols? My dear Peggy, I know nothing about such a man."

"He *is* murdered!" cried the girl in an agony.

"Will it make you happy to know that he is un-harmed?"

"Oh, heaven be praised!"

He appeared strangely moved. A touch of his knee, and Monsieur le Duc stepped close until the face of El Cantor was mere inches from the face of the girl. There swept over her the same feeling of weakness, of helplessness, which had come before when he was so very near.

"Look me fairly in the eye," commanded El Cantor.

She could not help but raise her head, no more than if a resistless hand compelled her.

"Tell me now, truly, what this man means to you, this Nichols. Tell me if you are very fond of him!"

"You would murder him then!"

"You are a silly child. If you love him, Peggy, I give you my sacred honor that he will be brought to you unharmed."

"Your honor!" sobbed the girl, in a burst of grief and helpless anguish.

"Do you think I am without it? You do not know me, my dear. You do not dream of the truth about me. You know me so little that you cannot understand that if you love this fellow truly, you are worthless to me.

"No, Peggy, if ever in your life you have truly loved another man and told him so, and let him take you in his arms, if you have so much as taken the serious thought of another man into your heart, you are no more to me than the dust in which my horse walks.

"And if that is true, I shall give you that money in the wallet—give it freely, do you understand? And leave you and this country and forget you as perfectly as a drunkard forgets his dream!"

It made her brain reel.

"You mean it!" breathed she. "You are sincere, John!"

They had forgotten the growing dusk, the very horses they sat upon, the dusky red which was fading along the horizon line, so filled were they with the study of each other. And even this first speaking of his given name came from her lips unregarded by either.

"I mean it with all my heart," said he. "I found you ice, my dear, but crystal-clear ice. Tell me, simply and truly, that there has been another man locked up in your heart all this time, and I release you absolutely. You may have that money as a gift, or as a business loan, or in any way in which it may be most acceptable to you. And this, I repeat, is on my honor!"

She made a vague gesture, as though she were trying to sketch before her the hugeness of this offer.

"And yet," she said, suddenly taken aback, "it means that you trust me!"

"More utterly than I trust myself!"

"And my mere word is enough to you?"

"Yes. Can you give it to me, Peggy? Can you tell me honestly that you have loved another man?"

The greatness of her hope flared in her eyes, for with a word she could snap all the power of his hold upon her. And it seemed to her, also, that staring up into his black eyes she saw his old surety crumble away.

"You see," said he, "that I know you better than you know yourself. You cannot lie to me, not even to save yourself. And on account of this, I swear to you that I respect you, Peggy, more than any woman was ever respected by a man before!"

She found her hand taken and raised. She saw his bared head bowed; she felt his lips upon her fingers. Then he was saying gravely: "Of course, you will choose to have the marriage ceremony as late as possible tomorrow. Suppose that I call for you at the parson's house, a little after eleven. The day ends at midnight, my dear, and the moment the last stroke has died away, I shall expect you to live up to your compact with me and allow the minister to begin the ceremony. I shall see to the license beforehand. Good night!"

He reined Monsieur le Duc away, making the beautiful creature bow to her like a circus horse. Cold desperation took hold on the girl.

"John Albert!" she cried.

He was beside her again instantly.

123

"You are not what I thought. You are a gentleman, John Albert! And being that, you cannot go on with this terrible thing. You would not force me to marry you, John! For dear mercy, you would not take me against my will!"

"Mercy?" said he, smiling down at her. "My dear child, mercy is beneath me. *I* despise it, and I despise the merciful. As for your obligation to me, I assure you solemnly that I shall extract the last scruple of fulfillment from you. If I should give you up, having done what I have already done, I should lose my self-respect, and rather than lose that, I would leap into a den filled with poisonous snakes.

"Mercy?" he repeated, with a quiver of his nostrils and a flare in his eye which seemed to her like a touch of actual madness. "Mercy? I shall show you the same order of mercy which *I* received when I was helpless and at the will of the world! Once more, adieu!"

And he was off with a rush of hoofbeats, a scattering of gravel that rattled about her. In the last glimmer of the day's light, the red bay glanced on the next hilltop, then dropped into blackness beyond.

15

Even the heat could not subdue the elation of Mr. Gorman. It forced him to issue from the house, every now and then, and sauntering back and forth from the house to the sheds, he thrust his hands deep in his trousers pockets, thus thrusting back his coat until his vest was revealed, heavily crossed by a great gold chain, every link of which was a fancifully shaped nugget. And there was also exposed a platinum fob with a single great diamond glittering in the center of it.

"There," he was fond of saying, "is a hundred steers boiled down rather small, eh?"

To-day, however, he felt that he had pushed to a successful conclusion his most Napoleonic coup. At noon, Lew Solway must sell, and the moment he accepted the check of Gorman, the banker secured at the same time infallibly the land of Henry Swain which lay between the Solway and Gorman places, without water except from them.

Here was emphatically something for nothing. And when he stared across those rolling, upland acres and made out the great splotch of greenery which surrounded the house of the tenderfoot rancher, Mr. Gorman could not suppress a smile.

"By twelve o'clock, Solway," he told the other, "everything that my eyes can see from this door is mine, or as good as mine! Unless," he added, "you'll sell before that hour."

Mr. Solway looked upon the purchaser of his ranch with a solemn disapproval.

"I'll wait until twelve," said he, "it ain't lackin' more'n an hour and a half—hardly that, I reckon?"

"An hour and twenty-two minutes," said the banker, snapping open a great gold watch. "But I'm willing to wait. A little haste—a little too much haste, Solway, has ruined a great many lives. A single slip may undo the work of years!"

"Like when a couple of thugs bust into a bank and grab over sixty thousand dollars?" suggested Solway maliciously.

Mr. Gorman turned purple.

"The devil has his innings now and then," he explained. "Who is that?"

He pointed to a dust cloud which was forming down the road.

"Maybe," said Solway without hope, "somebody that'll bid agin' you, Mr. Gorman."

"I suppose," smiled the banker, "that you'd give almost anyone else a lower figure than you've quoted to me?"

Solway said not a word, but he strained his desert-misted eyes through the window toward the house of his neighbor.

"Will you be moving into that place, Gorman?" he asked.

"The finest house in the country? Of course I'll take it. Why not?"

"I was only supposin' that some folks would figger on bein' troubled some by ghosts, Gorman. That was all."

This he remarked while throwing up a smoke screen with his pipe. Through the smoke the banker glanced with a look of venomous disapproval, but he could not afford to quarrel with the other at such a moment as this.

"'Damnation!" cried Solway. "It's the Swain girl comin'!"

"She's come to beg for her old man," the banker suggested, without particular discontent. "I guess he figures that's the last string in his bow. A pretty poor one."

Lew Solway favored his visitor with a deep sigh. "Doggone me, it ain't possible!"

"It's Peggy Swain, though," the banker declared, as she broke through the thin dust cloud and came clearly into view down the last slope. "And what else could bring her here?"

Lew Solway favored his vistor with a glance of undisguised disgust. Then he hurried to the door and down the steps in time to hold the stirrup of Margaret Swain

126

as she dismounted. He thought that her face was pale, but her eye was brighter than ever.

"If they was anything you might lack," suggested Solway miserably, "suppose you was to tell me out here? Because inside they's a gent that you ain't none too partial to, I take it. Gorman is inside, Miss Swain."

"Of course," said she, "this was to be his day. But I'm rather glad that he's here to learn my errand. Dear Mr. Solway, after the way you've held out for us and tried to help us, I know that you'll be glad, too!"

At this, he hastened into the house at her side, trembling with excitement. "You ain't meanin'—" he murmured under his breath.

Then he saw his two guests bowing to each other. Mr. Gorman was magnificently self-possessed.

"This," said the banker, "is a painful moment, I am sure, to both of us. To you on account of your poor father—to me because one must often regret what one is forced to do—forced, I may say, by one's business duties; one's duty to oneself!"

He was so pleased with this neat phrasing that he could not help smiling, although he bit his lip to keep from it. But the girl's own smile was wonderfully direct and unembarrassed.

"Of course I understand you," she declared. "But I think that father may forgive you for forcing us to buy Mr. Solway's place."

"For forcing you?" said Gorman, dumfounded.

"You've set a price, Mr. Solway?" she remarked, turning to the rancher.

"Seein' the way everything is, I might come down a thousand or two under sixty-five, Miss Swain," said that honest man.

"There is no need," answered the girl. "I've brought a cashier's check for the amount. I suppose it is the same as cash?"

127

Mr. Gorman raised a hand of protest—it was as though he was fumbling at a far-distant idea.

"Solway! Solway!" he cried. "If it's a matter of price —the matter of bucking it up a few thousands above sixty-five—considering the matter in all lights—"

"Considerin' the matter in all lights," said Solway, "when you looked things over you says to me that you'd pay me sixty-five thousand. That was all. Maybe I thought that the place was worth a hundred. Maybe some thought that it was worth a hundred and twenty. But sixty-five was all you could see your way clear to payin' for it. And sixty-five is what I sell for!"

"You've not gone mad, Solway," gasped the banker. "Heaven, man, you wouldn't turn down cold cash to the tune of a few extra thousands?"

"Sixty-five is what I was set on sellin' for, and sixty-five is what it goes for," replied Solway stubbornly.

"Now say that slow," said Gorman, scowling at the old man. "I want to hear that again. I offer seventy—but you intend to sell for sixty-five?"

Emotion made the voice and the very body of the old man quiver as he answered.

"I'll tell you the difference. Sixty-five thousand dollars from a white man is worth more'n ten times that many dollars from a yaller sneak and cutthroat. Gorman, I dunno how many folks has had a chance to tell you what they think of you.

"You got guns in your hands—dollars is guns to poor folks like the most of us. Now, I'm gonna tell you short and clean. Gorman, the reason why you always hated Swain was because he was big enough so he didn't have to crawl to you every season to get an advance for pullin' him through the winter.

"But I tell you, Gorman, that I'd rather sell to Swain and this here girl for sixty-five thousand than to you for a half a million. Now that's the fact. Will you swaller it?"

He had worked himself into a frenzy of anger. His body quaked with it. Only his right hand was steady as a rock as it reached behind him and gripped the butt of his gun.

There was no need to draw it. Mr. Gorman, having studied the anger and the coolness of the rancher for the most fleeting instant, rushed away through the door and gave his fury a vocalization in the open air. And, as he disappeared, Lew Solway was overwhelmed by the strangest event of his long and lonely life.

For he was caught in two strong young arms. He was kissed upon either cheek. And he found himself staring into glistening young eyes level with his own, so greatly had age stooped him from his prime!

"Dear Lew Solway!" she cried to him. "But you'll find that you haven't sold it. It's still your home. It's yours as much as it's dad's. For all he wants is a chance to exist. And so—God bless you!"

"It ain't nothin'!" said Solway, beginning to grow weak in his reaction. "Only seein' the way that a skunk like him had been walkin' up and down on the spines of real manfolks. Doggone me if it wasn't enough to peeve a doggone archangel!"

Back to the house of her father, with the flying mare straining every nerve to get on faster and faster, rushed Peggy Swain. She dared not move slowly, lest the horror which was swimming in the corners of her brain should sweep out and overshadow her.

She went to Henry Swain, at last, with a flush in her cheeks and her footfall feathery light, so that he looked up to her out of his hollow eyes like a fever patient who takes one breath of the sea breeze through the open window. She could not speak; she could only thrust into his hands the bill of sale which made the Solway place his own. He stared, he wondered over it, he was lifted to his feet by the realization of what it meant.

"Peggy!" he cried to her. "Does it mean that we're saved?"

"And your work safe!" she told him, half sobbing with her joy. "Your life of work saved to you, dad."

"Tell me how!"

She shook her head.

"It doesn't matter!"

"Peg, by heaven, you've done some desperate thing."

"No, no! This is our happy day. This is our day of salvation, and we mustn't let a shadow—"

He caught her firmly by the shoulders and drew her around so that the light from the window streamed full against her eyes. And from that position, with her head imprisoned, she could not avoid the inquisition of his glance. She quailed under it, and the horror from which she had been fleeing overtook her. He could see it as clearly as the lookout describes the landfall when he looks through the rift in the storm.

"What is it?" he asked her. "The ranch? Why, confound the ranch and my work. You're my work, Peg. I'd rather that ten thousand ranches were wiped out of existence than put a single shadow upon you. Now, what have you done?"

"What every woman does sooner or later. I've promised to marry—"

"Great Scott!" cried poor Henry Swain, loosing his hold on her, as if his strength were sapped suddenly from his entire body. "It's Hugh Nichols. That's the secret behind his coming. You've sold yourself—turned yourself into so much merchandise!"

"It's not he," she said drearily.

For if he raged so at the thought of even Hugh Nichols, well born, well bred, what would he have to say to the reckless young devil who had burned across the mind of Gloryville like a branding iron across the silken flank of a young steer?

130

"It's not Nichols?" echoed her father. "It's Garry Mason, then. By gad, it's the Mason boy. He's dropped his millions into the bidding and—"

She could not endure the length of the scene. And besides, every moment that she waited, she was seeing more and more clearly that grim future which lay before her.

"Dad, it's John Albert—"

"Who? It's who, Peg?"

"The man they call Jingle Bells."

Oh, to have had the strength to smile then, she would have given a great gift. But she had no strength. And she was heartsick as she knew that her despair was looking blankly at him out of her face.

"Jingle Bells? Jingle Bells?" he was saying over and over. "Not the Mexican vagabond! Not the gunfighting, man-killing bravo—not El Cantor, Peg? If he had such a sum of money as was needed to buy the Lew Solway place, it's stolen money. But in exchange for *you*, Peg?"

She had fought it back with a savage energy, but now self-pity, with an unnerving touch, undid her strength. Tears rushed into her eyes. Her lips began to tremble.

"For heaven's sake, Peg, to throw yourself away on a vagrant? I had rather put a bullet through my head than live an instant at the price of such an arrangement. But it isn't true. At least, you have't gone through the ceremony, Peg?"

"To-night," said she. "By twelve o'clock I'm to meet him at the parson's house. I've pledged my honor to him, dad!"

Here the tears broke and coursed down her cheeks. She fell into the arms of Henry Swain and clutched at him.

"Don't let him take me, dad! I'm afraid! I'm afraid! Don't let him take—"

She grew incoherent with sobbing. And before a passion of shame could come over her and stiffen her courage, Henry Swain picked her up and carried her to her room, and left her there on the bed, with the shade drawn. He sat beside her for a short moment, stroking her burning forehead, and his voice was softer and calmer than the sound of running water.

"I have to leave you to untangle this mess," said he. "It may take a little time. But you mustn't worry, my dear. Tush! These things don't happen in the twentieth century. They don't happen, Peg. Marriage as an article of commerce? Heaven bless me, what a yellow rat the man is! But drop all thought of it. Put the whole matter into my hands. Now rest, Peg! Poor Peg, my dear girl!"

He went out quietly; and in a moment more, as she lay huddled on the bed, trembling with an agony of remorse for her weakness, with a feeling that all that was splendid and strong in her had been broken forever, she heard the rush of the hoofs of a galloping horse down the driveway past the house and after that, her thought galloped at the side of her father toward the town of Gloryville.

But what could he do?

In the mind of Henry Swain there was only one thing. And that was, to do as his fighting ancestors would have done before him—meet the transgressor and beat him down. He went from his daughter straight to his room and took from the bureau drawer an old .44 caliber revolver. He had not touched it for six months, and then it had been merely to open it and discharge one chamber to see that all was well. Now he examined it hastily, dropped it into a pocket, and hurried for his horse.

He drove the big gelding hard. It was a-slather with thick, creaming foam when he reached Gloryville and reined in the tired, panting horse. Before the dust cloud was done boiling up around the spot where the gelding had skidded to a halt, Swain himself was crossing the hotel veranda.

He said to the portly proprietor, Hen Pearson: "I want this Jingle Bells, or by whatever name he may be known. Is he here?"

"Ain't seein' nobody," Pearson replied. "He's enjoyin' a siesta, maybe. That's his usual along in the middle of the day like this."

But Henry Swain waited to hear no more. He asked the number of the room, and in a trice he was before the door. Twice and again he knocked before it swung open before him and he found himself confronting Jingle Bells himself. He glanced hastily around among the shadows in the corners of the room. But the gigantic black was not there, and the rancher gained more confidence.

Besides, seen face to face in this fashion, Jingle Bells seemed astonishingly slender. He was hardly more brawny than a boy of fifteen. Indeed, the courage of the rancher increased a hundredfold. Jingle Bells greeted him very quietly. He was so matter of fact that Swain was dumfounded.

"You've learned the great news, I see," Jingle Bells remarked. "And you like it even less than I feared you would. Well, sir, all I can do is to say that I'm very sorry."

"Sorry?" said the other. "Sorry? Come, come, Mr. John Albert, if that is really your name—"

"It is not," said Jingle Bells frankly. "However, it will do for the nonce, so to speak."

"It will," the older man agreed. "I have come to confess to you, that if this is an elaborate jest, you have gone too far with it. My daughter is growing hysterical. But I have no doubt, Mr. Albert, that it *is* a jest. A man capable of doing what you have done in buying the Solway place is incapable of driving to a conclusion such a remarkable bargain as you have made with my girl."

"Do you think so?" smiled Jingle Bells. "Dear Mr. Swain, I fear that you will be like most fathers-in-law—without a stirring imagination."

The last of Mr. Swain's good humor had been used up some moments before.

"Or," said he, "if I am to understand that you have made the proposal seriously to her, I tell you that the affair can never be concluded in that fashion."

"Really?"

"Because, sir," cried Henry Swain, "it is impossible, it is revolting to nature that a rascal like you should ever call a woman like my daughter your wife!"

Here, then, was the insult, the gauntlet thrown down, and with his eyes starting, his face white, the beaded sweat standing on his brow and his body trembling, Swain gripped the butt of his revolver and prepared to kill or be killed.

Jingle Bells leaned forward, but it was only to smile into the face of the other.

"You are brave," he confessed, "but foolish. Do you seriously think that I shall murder you?"

"John Albert, unless you draw your gun, I swear I'll have you hounded out of the state by—"

Under the cold smile of Jingle Bells his protest died away.

"You are not convincing," declared Jingle Bells without emotion. "People will not believe that I have been afraid to meet a rusty old chap like you, though they may very well believe that I have refused to murder you."

He picked up, as he spoke, a little ash tray made of the entire shell of a tiny tortoise. The water lines in the shell had been picked out with silver, the broad mottled patterns on the back were done in gold, and the shell itself had been polished until it shone like glass. Having

134

lighted a cigarette he offered another to Swain.

But the rancher threw up his hands with a groan of shame and of grief. For he knew well enough that his interview had been a wretched fiasco. He might as well stand before the fatal lightning as stand before Jingle Bells. Destruction could not have been more certain. The scornful calm of the younger man was like acid in an open wound to Swain. He turned and fled from the room.

His brain was whirling now. By the time he reached the street, he had only one idea, and that was to call upon the vested powers of the law—call upon the sheriff himself, and see if the sheriff could not prevent this outrage. For prevented it must be.

He found Sheriff Walter Long at his house and dragged him instantly out into the open to hear a story too dreadful to be confided with the treachery of walls nearby. Then he talked without shame, while the sheriff leaned against the trunk of the only pear tree in Gloryville and filled his pipe and refilled it until the tobacco was tamped hard as a rock.

"There," said Swain, speaking as one too much tormented by great emotions to feel smaller ones. "There, Long, is the whole black story. He has the promise of my girl to marry him at the end of the day—that is to say, at midnight, and by heavens, the rat intends to keep her to her word. Walter Long, what can we do?"

"Give me ten minutes," the sheriff replied.

He took off his hat and sat down cross-legged in the shade of the tree. There he smoked until his quota of time was fully exhausted. At last he said: "They's only one thing to do, Swain. Gimme a charge to arrest him on, and I'll see that he sweats in the jail to-night."

"Give you one?" cried Swain. "Long, can't you invent a good reason in a cause like this?"

"Partner," grinned the sheriff, "I been tryin' for weeks

135

to pin someting on this here Jingle Bells—it's like tryin' to salt the tail of a wild duck!"

16

Sheriff Walter Long could smile in a manner which maddened poor Henry Swain, and sent him furiously away with a feeling that he had humiliated himself and his family in vain in opening his sorrow to the sheriff, but in his heart, Mr. Walter Long felt the tragedy as keenly as any one. Yet, after Mr. Swain departed, the honest sheriff remained for another full half hour over his pipe, lost in thought.

Then a thought touched him and made him stir as if a spur had pricked the skin. He finished his smoke, and his eyes were gleaming before he tapped the dottle out of his pipe. Yet he paused, still, to give the pipe a rub on his trousers and then admire the state of brown-black color and satin polish to which it had been brought by many years of patient smoking and pocket friction. For the sheriff was not a man of haste. He believed in the ways of the tortoise, and yet many and many a speeding hare he had caught!

When he arose, he went straight to the house of Señor Alvarez, and at the patio entrance he asked for the lord of the household. Alvarez was presently before him, sweating with haste, and a little pale. For visits from the sheriff of the county did not come every day and perhaps there were certain little features of Alvarez's business, connected with affairs across the southern border, which prevented him from welcoming the presence of the law. But the sheriff hastened to put him at ease.

"Alvarez," said he, "I'm here tryin' to get information from one of your family. I need that information to make an arrest, and the one I want to talk to is the señorita."

The color surged back into the face of the man of wealth. And a shadow rolled across his brow.

"Alicia," he stated gloomily, "is not well."

And he stared at the floor.

"Why," said the sheriff, grinning broadly, "d' you think that I'll be runnin' off with her, man? Not while Mrs. Walter Long is alive to hear about it. But I have to talk with her, Alvarez. I think she may tell me things which will be of help in lodging a certain rascal behind the bars. Whisht, man—I mean El Cantor himself!"

It was the open sesame to the heart of Señor Alvarez. Sunshine returned to his face at once.

"Señor Sheriff," said he, "that murderer needs hanging. I shall send down Alicia to you at once. You shall talk with her alone. But one word first, if you hint at your business, I'm afraid—"

"Leave that to me," the sheriff declared. "I think that I have a way of making her talk."

In two minutes he sat in the cool shadows of the patio with the fountain showering near by, and the gold-green-and-crimson cockatoo eying him askance from its perch; then out came Alicia—and she came alone. She was all in black with one defiant red rose in her hair, and her head high.

Cautious politics, he decided, would never serve him here. He could not outmaneuver the subtle wits of this girl, no matter how he strove, so he said bluntly: "Señorita Alvarez, I have come here on an unpleasant errand. I'm lookin', between you and me, for a man-sized excuse to

137

arrest a man, and I dunno but that you could fix it for me, because you might know him better'n anybody else in town does. I'm talkin' about El Cantor, or Jingle Bells, or whatever name he gives himself!"

Her effrontery was matchless. She turned her soft, large eyes upon him with no more expression than lives in the eyes of a cat when he sits on the window sill and stares through the pane at the silent blackness of the night beyond. So Alicia looked at the sheriff.

"I have seen Señor El Cantor," she said. "I suppose every one in Gloryville saw him the day he arrived. All," she added sweetly, "except you, Señor Sheriff!"

There was a little sting in this remark which did not escape the sheriff. What a child she was, and yet what a woman already! She had unfurled a fan covered with gilded arabesques, a fan of transparent ivory, yellow with time. She began to cool herself with it, turning it with a round, childish wrist. But the sheriff understood it was rather as a screen against his prying eyes in case of need than to raise an air that she used it.

"I was away when he come," he admitted. "I was away, sort of hopin' that Sladen and Yarnell would have a chance to fight it out. When I came into town ag'in, I heard about the explosion that kept 'em apart. Well, señorita, Jingle Bells ain't been sittin' still all the time since then. He's been sort of busy."

"I do not know, señor," she remarked, "why you should tell me all this?"

The sheriff was wise enough merely to smile, and his smile brought a flush to the cheek of the girl, which she covered with a ready play of the fan again.

"However," said Long, "it ain't troublin' us, what he does with his time by day or by night. It ain't nothin' to us where he camps out, or where he sings."

The fan flickered for an instant in front of the eyes of the girl. Then she stared calmly forth upon the sheriff.

"So long as the trouble that gent makes bothers nobody but himself," announced the sheriff, "and so long as we ain't got no proofs agin' him, we don't care so much. But when he gets to mixin' around with the ladies, it's different."

"Ah," said Alicia indifferently, "this is pleasant gossip, Señor Sheriff."

She yawned a little, and her eyes were as ever, like the expressionless eyes of a cat which see everything, and reveal nothing.

"Now," said the sheriff, "we know that he's been comin' to see you."

The fan hesitated, and then paused. She stared straight at him without a word.

He went on smoothly: "Which there ain't no reason why you shouldn't see him. He's an amusin' rascal. As far back as we can trace him, he's been puttin' in a large slice of his time with the ladies. But when it comes to forcin' a lady to marry him, as he's doin' to-day with Margaret Swain—"

"Señor!" breathed Alicia.

"That's it," said Long. "I knowed that a smart girl like you would see through him. Amusin' but a rascal. That's the trouble with him.

"Well, what I was thinkin' was that somewheres out of your talk with him you might be able to think of somethin' that would do as an excuse to let me jail him. I wouldn't ask for much. But sometimes when a gent is talkin' to a lady, he gives his tongue its head and lets it run."

"He is to marry?" asked Alicia, with a glimmering lightning striking across her eyes, but with her voice as soft as ever.

"He has cornered her and bargained her into it. He's got her promise. It's over with, señorita, unless we can put him behind the bars."

"It is a trick!" gasped Alicia. "It is a trick to make me talk!"

"D'you think that?" Walter Long protested.

"Lady, I tell you that Margaret Swain is due at the parson's house—"

"Ah," cried the girl, suddenly convinced, "the lying demon! If I could—"

She checked herself.

"Where is Don Mateo? Find Don Mateo, señor."

"I seen him in the street two minutes back."

"Bring him to me. Jingle Bells would marry the Señorita Swain? It is because I pity her, señor. Do you understand?"

"Why," said the sheriff, "they ain't no other reason. You'd save her from hell-fire if you could. It's common charity, and that's all."

"Don Mateo, if he talks—"

"You mean, he's been smoked up a bit in the same kind of a fire? Señorita, what he tells me is State's evidence. There ain't no harm could come to him."

"Then bring him to me quickly—quickly!"

Walter Long waited for no more. He was out of the house and hurrying down the street to the general merchandise store in front of which he found Don Mateo in the very act of putting his foot into the stirrup. The Mexican youth turned yellow with fear when the hand of the sheriff fell on his shoulder.

"It's Alicia Alvarez," said Long. "She's aimin' to have a talk with you, Don Mateo."

Then, as he saw the gleaming eyes of the boy turned desperately toward the distant horizon, and fiercely back at the sheriff, the latter went on: "There ain't no call for fightin', Don Mateo. No harm comes your way. All you got to do is to tell what Alicia herself wants you to talk about. What I do is to sit by and listen, and that's all. And what we want is enough to land this here Jingle Bells in jail. That's all that we are after!"

Don Mateo answered nothing. But, very pale still, and very thoughtful, he removed his foot from the stirrup, tethered his horse at the rack once more, and turned away with the sheriff.

"The jail?" he repeated at last. "The jail for him? It is impossible!"

"Why," remarked the sheriff, "he'd look uncommon fine in stripes. He'd wear 'em like dinner clothes, he would!"

"Look, señor!"

He pointed to a hawk, stooping like a down-flung javelin over Gloryville.

"Can you imagine that hawk hung in a cage like a canary, Señor Long?"

17

All that Hugh Nichols could see of the world was observed through the open door of the shack which served as his prison. As for the little window, it was securely boarded up by the last occupant of the shanty to keep out the prying fingers of the cold winter winds.

Through the doorway, however, he could look out to a wide sweep of blue sky, which had been pale with the fiery heat of the sun all the day and which was now dull with the evening, and turning to a deep and deeper blue, crossed with clouds startling white.

His view of all but the sky was very largely blocked by the enormous figure of his jailer who sat cross-legged on the threshold. Yet when the monster shifted now and again, Nichols caught glimpses down the hillside of a pleasant valley, crowded with pines over which the dust of the summer had sifted.

"I really don't see," said he, "what harm will be done if you allow me to sit in the doorway, or even a little outside."

He had made the same request before, and he had never gained any response. But his continual good nature had so far won upon the huge black, for the latter had long since discarded the mask which covered his face, that now Little Samuel replied: "What you ain't seein' you ain't wantin'. Settin' in there you rest pretty comfortable. You got a pile of straw to lie on, you got fine chuck to eat, and all you got to do is to snooze whenever you want to, and wake up hungry, and eat ag'in!

"But if you was to set out here, you'd be smellin' of the wind and wonderin' where it was bound for. And you'd be lookin' at the trees, and wonderin' where the first trail led to. And pretty soon, from wantin' to be gone, you'd be tryin' to be gone. And I sure would hate, mister, to be puncturin' you and drilling you all full of holes. Here we sit plumb peaceable and friendly. Why can't we stay this here way?"

So saying he heaved his head around on his thick neck, and bestowed his terrific grin upon his prisoner. Hugh Nichols sighed and submitted. It did not matter that his heart was breaking to be out and away.

It did not matter that, every instant, the picture of the girl grew larger and larger, and brighter and brighter in his eye, and that he groaned inwardly when he thought

142

how she must doubt him. He must show none of his emotion to his keeper. For the sight of his angry impatience would double the precautions of the latter.

Hitherto those precautions had grown less and less with the passing of every moment. When they arrived at the shack, Little Samuel had tied both the hands and the feet of Nichols, and had allowed him the use of only one free hand for the purpose of eating, and now and again smoking. That night, he had slept with his own left hand tied to the hands of his prisoner.

But after the morning had brightened, repose appeared to take away the suspicions of the black man. Eventually he freed the hands and feet of his captive; and finally Little Samuel sat at the door with his back turned upon him.

There was nothing within the bare little shack which Nichols could use as a weapon. A dozen times he had nerved himself to leap at his guard and clap a strangle hold upon his throat. He had won no little fame in three sports in his college days.

Yet, when he came to the verge of attacking Little Samuel, he hesitated and then gave up the job. For it was like attacking a wild beast. The enormous back of the black man, bulging with muscles, his neck like the trunk of an oak tree, his long, thick arms gave promise of a power that could brush off all the science and all the strength of Nichols, and break him like matchwood.

Yet the desperation of the white man was growing. Evening was closing on his last day, and in the coming of the dark he felt an end of his hopes of ever reaching the girl. The ruin of her father would be completed and his hope of winning her more-than-golden gratitude was lost.

Little Samuel was thrumming lightly on his banjo, monotonously, over and over, the same tune. It seemed to Nichols that he would go mad if the noise did not cease. His horse, tethered behind the shack, interrupted the playing for a moment by dragging at some of the grass which grew long about the baseboards of the shanty. Little Samuel drove the animal away with a curse and a shout. Then the thrumming began again, the big man swaying rhythmically to the unsung words and unsung tune.

"Well," said Nichols at last, "I don't suppose you sing?"

"Sing, mister?" Little Samuel remarked jerking his head around again until his smile gleamed white at his prisoner. "That's somethin' that I can't do nothin' else besides. I was born singin', and I'll die singin'. Some folks is full of ructions and hell-fire, like him that makes me keep you here. Some folks is full of the hankerin' after money. some folks is full of meanness, and some folks is full of smiles, but me, Mr. Nichols, I'm full of song. It jest comes out nacheral, doggone my hide!"

He laughed softly with the joy of that thought, laughed until the shanty quivered with his mirth and his self-content.

"Very well," Nichols suggested, "there's no harm in trying one."

"Might you be a-hankerin' after music all of this time?" said the genial Samuel. "Why sir, I been hankerin' to sing, but I didn't know what your tastes might be. Well, sir, here's the story of how El Cantor he come down from Mesa Grande to the Rio in two days, ridin' Monsieur le Duc. You've heard tell about Monsieur le Duc, I reckon?"

"About whom?"

"The hoss that El Cantor rides."

"No. I have never even heard of El Cantor, as a matter of fact. Is he an Indian chief, or some such personage?"

"Injun?" snorted Little Samuel. "Well, sir, maybe you'll have a chance to get to know him a pile better one of these here days. He's like his hoss, and they ain't another hoss like Monsieur le Duc in the world. Take a wild mustang stallion, or a thoroughbred, and stake 'em along Monsieur le Duc, and they ain't worth lookin' at. Take a gunfightin' crook, or a slick Down East sharper, or a doggone fine upstandin' gentleman and stack 'em alongside of El Cantor and they don't look like nothin'!"

There flashed across the mind of Nichols the strangely beautiful outline of the horse which he had seen blackened against the sunset the night before. He began to take a keener interest in El Cantor and his affairs.

In the meantime, Little Samuel rolled back his head, struck the banjo into a noisy ecstasy, and thundered forth a long ballad of how the red bay had strode across the hot desert miles from Mesa Grande to the Rio bearing El Cantor upon his back. So huge was that voice, flooding thickly through the narrow confines of the little shack, that Nichols was at first almost deafened.

Then, as he watched Little Samuel rolling from side to side, carried away by a musical frenzy, Hugh Nichols grew grave with another thought. That roar of harmony was like the thunder of a waterfall. It would quite drown all other ordinary sounds.

And Nichols, tentatively, stretched forth his hand and pressed one of the boards which formed the wall of the shack. It was loose past belief! At the first thrust, it gave way at one end, the rust-rotted nails breaking off at the head.

He tried the board above it. This time there was a greater effort needed, and the nails made a dangerous creaking, but even that sound was lost in the mellow thunder of Little Samuel's singing. Here were two boards, then, hanging by one end only, and from that poor support sagging sadly. One more thrust of the hand would break them both away and leave a space through which a man could crawl easily.

But before he could touch the board again, the tale

145

of El Cantor ended with the triumphant rider safely across the Rio Grande, and Little Samuel turned his head for applause.

How could his eye fail to see that gaping hole which was opening in the back wall of the shack? Nichols strove to turn him back to his instrument with commendation.

"That's a fine piece of work," he declared. "Where did you find the music and the words?"

"Right out of my own head," the giant replied, grinning broadly, and so tickled to the heart that he was blinded by vanity. "Them words I picked up, and that there music was jiggin' around inside of my head waitin' for a chance to come out."

"That's rare," said Nichols. "But after all, that's a short song."

"Short and long," Little Samuel announced, "they came nacheral to me. Here, you might say, is a tolerable long one."

With that, he inclined his enormous head back again and sang another.

When the ballad maker was well under way in his performance, Nichols tried the upper board stealthily with his hand. It required a stiff pressure before it yielded. But now it was gone. He started on the lower board. It came away almost at a touch as its other end had done. Certainly the old shack was on the verge of falling to pieces, and the next touch of winter would bring it down.

He flattened himself against the floor and looked out. Yonder was the horse on which he had been mounted by those treacherous companions who escorted him from the train—a well-made animal, securely hobbled.

Hugh Nichols glided through the aperture. From the outside, he cast one glance back at the bulk of his captor where he sat in the doorway, swaying slowly with the rhythm of his music, quivering with the joy of his composition and his rendering of it.

146

Nichols was instantly beside the horse. The knot of the hobble held stubbornly against his struggling fingers. But that was only for a moment. Then, with the loosed rope in his hands, he tied it around the neck of the gentle animal, and passed a loop over its nose. In this way he had ridden a good-natured saddle horse in his boyhood, and perhaps he could ride even this desert-trained mount.

He leaped to its back, at which it reared straight up and he had to hold to its mane to keep it from sliding him off over its tail. And the voice of the singer bellowed on still.

The horse started away down the slope, first at a walk, then at a soft trot, but constantly prying at the rope with his head, as though expectant of the stern control of bits and bridle reins, and astonished to be checked, instead, only by the mild pull of the rope around its head.

The gelding, sensing his freedom, broke into a full gallop with such a clattering among the stones that the singer broke off short. Then a wild yell of astonishment and of rage roared from the throat of Little Samuel.

He leaped to his feet and hurried around the corner of the shack, gun in hand. The revolver barked, and a bullet whistled over the head of Hugh Nichols. The next instant his speeding horse had carried him into the screening pines, and he was safe.

Safe from the black he was, but not safe from the very horse which was his engine of deliverance. The gelding was now racing frantically, throwing in a little buck jump now and then to unseat his passenger, or swerving under the lower limbs of the trees to brush him off.

But Nichols flattened himself along the back of the horse. He avoided the lower limbs in this way, and as for the whipping of the smaller ones, he cared not for that. This was a small price to pay. At least he was freed, and headed in the general direction of the ranch of Henry Swain, as nearly as he could tell.

Then the first burst of fury and of joy left the horse. It began to go on with a more measured pace, taking the hills at a trot, only galloping across the level or the gentle down slopes. It had given up all hope of unseating its rider; it would have answered the guiding hand of Nichols, but the rider dared not use his own sense of direction. Far better, he felt, to permit the horse to go his own way.

It appeared to him, sometimes, that they were traveling in a broad circle. Again and again he fought back an impulse to twitch the rope, but he controlled that desire. He contented himself finally with merely urging the horse forward with greater speed along the road which it itself selected.

Now, from time to time, he consulted his watch. It was growing late, and very late. It was ten, and half past. It was eleven, and after. Then he saw, before him, the broad belt of the river's face, shimmering in the light of the stars. A little more, and a sprinkling of lights—a town was just before him!

He struck the flank of the gelding a sharp blow with the rope. It rocked away into a swinging, weary canter that rushed him closer and closer to the village. At the first house he saw on the veranda the rudely outlined forms of a man and a woman seated on the steps. He jerked the gelding to a halt.

"What town is this?" cried Nichols.

There was a pause, and then a startled response: "Gloryville!"

It was like a word of salvation to Hugh Nichols. For during the last two hours he had been more than half persuaded that the horse was carrying him in the opposite of the right direction.

148

"My friend," he called again, "can you tell me the road to the Henry Swain place?"

Here the girl answered: "D'you want Mr. Swain?"

"His daughter."

"Her? Well, they're both at the parson's house."

"The parson's house!"

"The talk is she's to get married. They're waitin' up. I dunno why!"

"Married?" groaned Nichols. "Where is that house?"

"Yonder. Right down the street. You can see that lighted window, the only one on the other side—"

He was off like a flash, jerked at his gelding to slow its pace, and so shot to the ground and ran through the gate of the parsonage and fairly into the arms of two men, who gripped him on either side while a third jammed a gun at his head.

"Good heavens!" cried Nichols. "The whole world is mad!"

"It ain't him," said a strong, nasal voice. "It ain't Jingle Bells after all. Who are you, young fellow?"

"I am Hugh Nichols!"

"Hugh Nichols?" exclaimed another. "Nichols, I am Henry Swain. Sheriff, let this man go. He is my friend and the friend of Peggy.

"Nichols," he added, working through to the other and finding his hand in the darkness, "we have been terribly anxious about you. The two men we sent to escort you returned wounded—you failed to arrive— we were afraid that there had been a murder—"

"I can tell you a story," said Nichols, "that sounds like something out of the Arabian Nights, of how I was bound by my two guides who came for me, and then carried away after my pockets had been looted—carried away and guarded by the biggest black I ever saw—a giant."

"Little Samuel!" exclaimed the sheriff. "It works out as

149

perfectly as any circle. There is the hand of Jingle Bells in the whole thing. but this time he has blundered—one thing goes wrong—everything goes wrong!"

"I want to find Margaret Swain," Nichols declared, greatly excited. "I want her to understand—"

"Steady, Nichols," said Henry Swain. "Let me tell you that it is best that you should not face her suddenly. She has told me of the fine thing you attempted to do for me in bringing down help. Whether you succeeded or not makes not a bit of difference in my appreciation, but Peggy is in a strange predicament.

"She managed this whole affair from the first without consulting me, of course, and finally she got help—got it from a villain, the same one who had you waylaid, the same one who shot down my two men, the man called El Cantor, Jingle Bells, John Albert, Slim Jim, Miss Mañana—and a dozen other names. That's the fellow, Nichols, who got the help I needed, and she bargained herself away for the loan!

"Man, she swore she would marry the rascal unless the money arrived to pay him back, and it was to repay him that you were to come in in her scheme."

"And I *shall* repay the scoundrel!" cried Hugh Nichols. "And crack his skull for him afterward!"

"It's too late to repay him," said Henry Swain. "There is no bank open, even if it could cash a check for sixty-five thousand dollars, which it could not do, of course! There is nothing for my girl to do except to sit in that room, yonder, and wait for midnight, because it is at that moment that the day ends and it is at that time that he is sure to come to claim her. There she sits and waits for him, and the parson is with her, talking nonsense with her while her heart is breaking. There she sits, ready for her martyrdom, and quite game to go through with it.

150

"But in the meantime we have enough information to warrant the arrest of the wretch, and here we wait, sure of him at last, Nichols, perfectly certain to take him the instant he comes to take the girl. And there you are—as neat a little drama as ever was played. My only regret is that the money of this young demon—stolen money, I have no doubt—has been used to help me. I'd repay it with drops of blood if I could. But since I cannot do that I must, nevertheless, see to it that his mad scheme does not go through.

"And there, Nichols, is the whole story. Only, I beg you not to see Peggy now. It would break her down. She's devilish fond of you, my boy. You can see her through the window, yonder, chatting with the parson and smiling as cool as you please but as white as linen, by gad, poor girl. Stay out here with us, Nichols, and if the fish rises, help us to land it."

"With all my heart," said Hugh Nichols. "But this is like joining an army. How many are they here—eight men?"

"We may need them all. He's a tiger, this El Cantor. But we're sure to get him. He'll try to reach my girl. And he hasn't been seen around Gloryville all of today. He must come in. And when he comes in, guard every possible approach to the house and even to the old shed yonder which connects with it from behind.

"Nichols, we have quietly stowed away more than a dozen men near here, and every one is a fighter. And yonder, by good luck, rises the moon to watch us!"

151

18

That same moon, at that very moment, was stealing across the upper floor of the old cattle shed which, after the New England fashion, was built in connection with the dwelling house. And as it slipped over the floor, polished by the shifting of many and many a ton of loose hay, it touched the shadowy form of a sleeper and then reached his face just as the church bell, around the corner from the house, began to chime, striking out the notes singly and sending them in humming waves through the night.

At the first sound of the bell the sleeper stirred; at the second he sat bolt upright and then started to his feet, where he yawned and stretched deliberately and, turning to the window, showed the handsome face and the bright, dark eyes of El Cantor himself.

He sat down again, cross-legged, and, drawing out a little rectangular pocket mirror, went on to make his toilet, brushing his hair, dusting his clothes, and working for some moments industriously. The midnight clock had ceased ringing before he was ended with his toilet. Then he went to the window and stood there for a moment breathing deeply the cool air of the night and letting his senses come gradually back to normal.

When he was fully wakened, he started for the parsonage, not as a man would go, but as a cat might travel. That is to say, he was out the window in a trice, and so across the roof to the main roof of the house, over this softly and smoothly, in spite of the dangerous slope to the dormer window. This was locked, but a moment of manipulation with the slender blade of a knife turned the latch and presently he was in the house.

He paused and looked out the window to make sure again of certain observations which he had previously made from the window of the barn. There could be no mistake now. On the inside of the hedge which crossed the house in front, he saw dimly silhouetted the forms of three men, one of them carrying a shotgun, the other two with revolvers belted around their hips. But the shotgun meant a great deal. Men do not take to such weapons unless they are ready to shoot to kill.

El Cantor, leaning in the little attic window, considered those three men gravely, weighed his chances, and decided with perfect coolness and with perfect gravity that he had about one chance in three. However, he was used to odds even greater than these. Therefore, he went straightway down the stairs, and through the second story.

A dark form loomed suddenly before him, and a voice growled: "Hello—who's that?"

The hand of El Cantor closed on the butt of a knife. One quick thrust would silence this man's tongue, but another consideration made him pause as it had made him pause a hundred times before in his adventures. It was not a generous impulse. It was not a kindly regard for others.

It was simply a cold realization that murder does not pay and that in the end blood must be paid for with blood. It was therefore that he had gone on his way leaving so few red marks against him. It was therefore now that his hand left the butt of the knife.

"I been up on the roof," said he, sliding easily into the vernacular. "I been ridin' herd on the doggone moonshine till I'm tired. I'm gonna let the old man send up another shift."

He was pressing on even as he spoke, and the other let him go, merely muttering: "What's your name, partner? I dunno that I place your voice!"

153

But by this time, still whispering a wordless reply, El Cantor was on the stairway to the first floor, and he went steadily down it without a pause, without hurrying. He was not followed. And eventually he stood at the door of the parson's living room.

Here he waited, his face black, his jaw set, while he listened to the voices inside. The parson was talking drowsily; the girl was answering with monosyllables.

All that was savage in the heart of El Cantor was roused now. For he knew that the trap was set for him and he was certain that the girl had laid the plan for his capture. And at the thought of this treason he was cold with rage. Yet he waited at the door for a moment to gain some confirmation.

"It is too late, my dear child. This man will never come! He would have been here before, if he had intended coming."

"Ah, Mr. Clary," said a voice so changed that El Cantor could hardly recognize it, "he will come. I am as sure of him as I am sure of fate. Not that he wants me, really, but because he wishes to show the rest of the world that he can beat it, outwit it, make a fool of it when he pleases. That is what is in his brain! And he will come, Mr. Clary!"

"We will wait another half hour, then," the parson decided gravely. "But, Miss Swain you are making a great mistake—a very great mistake. You have already quarreled with your father about this."

"He would not have let me come," said she. "But I am of age. I have a right to a will of my own—I have an honor of my own. My honor was pledged, you know."

"The world must never know all of this," the parson declared in a troubled voice. "I sit here turning the question back and forth in my mind. What is just in the eyes of heaven I cannot tell, but it seems to me that since you have pledged yourself you must be true to your pledge. Otherwise, the world could not stand firm. I hope that

154

you are right, and if this strange, evil man insists, you must marry him."

"I must marry him!" sighed the girl.

El Cantor, beyond the door, felt his brain whirling around so fast that he had to put out a hand and lean against the wall for a moment until his thoughts were more ordered again. Then he raised his head slowly. There could be no doubt, from what he had heard her say, that she was there in good faith. If there were a trap set she was the bait without being aware of it.

In the darkness El Cantor smiled slowly, and a great weight slid from his heart. After all, it could be explained quite easily. Her father, having striven in vain to persuade her from this folly, had taken the matter into his own hands without letting her know of it.

He turned the knob of the door softly, carefully, but in spite of his care, there was a faint moan audible from the interior of the room. One of them had been watching that door and had seen the knob turned. El Cantor cast open the door quickly, and closed it again behind him as he stepped in.

It was the girl who had seen at once. She had leaped from her chair and stood before him now with a white face and the eyes of one who is going mad with fear. The parson, good old man that he was, paid not so much as the honor of a glance to the stranger. He started up and went to the girl to steady her, saying: "Now, my dear, be brave. You must keep a tight grip on yourself if you expect to go through with this!"

She nodded to him without taking her eyes from the handsome features of El Cantor and to his death day that look of hers would be printed in his mind.

"I shall not be foolish," said she. "I shall be steady enough."

"You are the man named John Albert?" said the parson, turning to his new guest, who had come in without being announced, and regarding him in such a fashion as might have withered the very soul of El Cantor. "You are John Albert? And you have come to marry Margaret Swain?"

El Cantor, slowly dragging off his hat, nodded.

"That is all true," he answered.

"My friend," said old Mr. Clary, "I suppose that you have meditated on the sin of this forced marriage in which you treat a gentle and noble girl like an article of merchandise? You, I hope, have thought of that?"

"I have thought of all that," El Cantor replied quietly. "Lock that door, if you please. We do not wish to be interrupted during the ceremony and there are a few friends of mine in Gloryville who might wish to make a noise if they knew what was happening. I suppose that would surprise you, Reverend Mr. Clary?"

The minister regarded him with bewilderment mixed with horror.

"I have no idea of what you are talking," he said dryly, but, nevertheless, locking the door on the farther side of the room. "If this thing must be done, however, I hope that there is to be no indecent haste?"

El Cantor was watching the windows. There were two of them on the same wall, and the shades of both were high, both were open and let in gusts of desert-warmed wind. Shadows, it seemed to El Cantor, were stirring beyond those windows.

"There is apt to be more haste than you imagine!" said El Cantor. "And as for decent deliberation, let it be damned. I am here to be married, and I presume that I have barely three minutes for the performance of that rite. Peggy will you draw those shades? I have an objection to letting myself be seen at those windows."

She stared at him, conjecture big in her face. Then she went to the first window without a word, lowered it, and drew down the shade. El Cantor, in the meantime, had crouched in the corner close to the floor, but he

156

suddenly exclaimed: "The devils have seen me!" and at the same time leaped sidewise on hands and feet, like a great, active ape, while a voice sang out close to the second window: "He's inside! He's inside, boys!"

At the same time a gun barked, and smashed through the wall just where El Cantor had been crouched. The long revolver slid into the hand of Jingle Bells. It exploded twice, with the muzzle turned upward. At the first shot the flame leaped in the throat of the oil lamp; at the second shot it went out. That old trick of shooting out the lights which had saved many a rascal in the earliest frontier days might serve Jingle Bells in this emergency.

The parson had shouted with terror at the explosion of the first gun. Then his voice rang wailing through the night: "For heaven's sake, men, no shooting! There is a woman in this room!"

"Open the doors, then!" shouted the familiar voice of the sheriff. "Open the doors, Clary. This one is locked!"

"One minute," cried the minister. "I shall have it open directly."

He was hurrying toward it when the hand of El Cantor gripped his shoulder and halted him.

19

"What is it?" gasped the Reverend Mr. Clary. "Do you hear them calling me, Mr. Albert?"

"I shall answer for you, however," said El Cantor.

"You will stay here, my friend, and the door is not to be opened. The door is not to be opened!"

He repeated it solemnly, then he called loudly: "Gentlemen, this is El Cantor, alias Jingle Bells!"

A shout of anger and of triumph answered him; then a voice rang in his ear.

"And this is Hugh Nichols! Do you hear me? There is a score between us which shall be settled if ever I have thirty seconds alone with you!"

"Hugh Nichols!" cried Peggy Swain.

"You've ended your dance, Jingle Bells," said the sheriff outside the door. "You might as well let us in. I'll tell you this: What we have against you is not murder. Matter of fact, it's something that might even be settled out of court. Will you listen to reason, Jingle Bells?"

"Mr. Long," El Cantor replied, "I trust that you will put some credit in what I have to say when I swear to you that if there is a noise again at either of those doors, I shall begin shooting through them. Will you believe me?"

"He's gonna hang himself before he gets through with it, and it ain't gonna be long before he's through," said one of those near the sheriff.

And another added: "Why not haul off and go slam through the door? Maybe he wouldn't get none of us!"

The sheriff regarded these speakers with a sort of sublime contempt; and without a word to them, as if what they had had to say was really not worthy of any answer other than silence, he turned to his own thoughts.

As for Señor Jingle Bells, he had slipped across the room after speaking, and knelt beside the door with his ear pressed to the crack so that he could hear whatever murmurs were nearest. Of one thing he was sure, having listened to the mumbled proposals for making a rush— that the sheriff was not yet keyed to the point at which he would be willing to take such a desperate chance.

Then he arose and glided back.

"Peggy!" he called in a loud whisper.

She came to him without a word. He felt the touch of her hand lightly on his arm and a light, light fragrance of her hair beside him.

"We are about to begin and go through with the thing," he told her.

He added in another whisper: "Clary!"

There was a faint groan from the minister.

"You start the wedding service now."

"Blasphemy!" groaned the poor minister.

"Do you hear me? Begin!"

The voice of the minister answered: "Does any person in this presence know any reason—"

"Not too loudly!" cautioned El Cantor.

"Ah, man," groaned the minister, "I fear that you are putting a cross against your name in the sight of heaven!"

"That may be. I shall take my chance of heaven after I have this girl. Continue!"

"Young man, I cannot and I shall not!"

"By the Eternal!" cried El Cantor, "I shall make that sure first. Do you think, old man, that I would stop at anything, having gone as far as this? Continue with the service."

"Our Father in Heaven forgive me!" breathed John Clary. "I shall be murdered if I do not!"

He repeated the last sentence hastily.

"Does any person in this presence know any reason why this man and woman should not be joined in the bonds of holy matrimony? If so, speak or forever hold your peace!"

Here there was a crash at the right-hand door leading into the room. Instantly the gun which was balanced in the hand of El Cantor exploded and was answered by a scream at the farther side of the door, followed by a wild scrambling and roars of rage and fear.

In the black of the room, the shriek of the terrified girl was like a sudden flare of blinding light. It made the minister himself cry out aloud.

"Steady, steady!" urged El Cantor. "I fired high. They only heard the hum of the bullet and thought they were dead men. They are a crowd of cowards and fools, Peggy. Confound them, they are not worth a thought from you."

"I am quite able to stand," said she coldly. "I do not need your hand."

"Very well, now—"

Here all sound of voices was drowned by a fresh clamoring outside the house.

"Go on!" commanded El Cantor. "The entire town is up now and packed around the parson's house. Man, man, do you think that I can wait here all night?"

"Repeat, after me," said John Clary, "I, John, take thee, Mary—heaven make me strong!" broke in the minister. "I cannot say it—I shall not say it, not though I am murdered for it. I shall not say it without the consent of the lady."

"Do you consent, Peggy?" asked El Cantor hoarsely.

"Yes."

He added in a sort of frenzy: "Do you hear me? You have only to say no, and I shall give you up. One syllable, one breath from you is enough to put an end to all of this!"

"Not a single word from me!" the girl replied. "I shall do what I have promised to do. To the last letter! I have given you my word of honor, John!"

"Repeat after me," said the minister again. "I, John, take thee, Mary—"

"No, no!" exclaimed El Cantor suddenly. "I thought I could do it—half for the devil that is in me, and half for the sake of laughing at them all, but I cannot, Peggy.

160

There is one woman in the world, and no more. There is one woman in the world, and that is you, Peggy!

"D'you hear me? You are free from your promise. You are perfectly safe and free! I give you up and all the claim that I had upon you, which was never any real hold at all."

"Young man, young man!" exclaimed the minister, "who will say that there is no power in prayer or that I have not been heard by our Father? As for you, John Albert you will live to bless the day—"

"Old fool," said the irreverent El Cantor, "will you be quiet? Peggy, I want you to understand before I leave you. It is not fear of those dolts and clods outside the door. They are nothing to me. A million of them could not keep me from marrying you.

"But it is because I love you. I love you with such a will to own you freely, that I could not touch so much as the hem of your skirt without your willingness. Only this once, Peggy, to hold you close, to dream for an instant that you are mine—so, good-by!"

He sprang back from her. The shout of the sheriff was beating through the wall.

"Jingle Bells, we've made up our minds to the sacrifice. You may wound one or two of us, you may even kill one or two of us, but it's not to be said that Gloryville was ever bluffed back by one man. We're going to break down that door, man, which is just in front of us here, and after we get inside, we're going to tear you to pieces if you've pulled a trigger. Do you understand me?"

"Sheriff," cried Jingle Bells, "if you try it, this room is going to run blood. I warn you!"

"Is that final?"

"It is!"

"Then heaven have mercy on you, Jingle Bells, because we'll have none! Boys, will you stand by me? Are you ready to take a hand?"

"Keep back, sheriff," came the strong voice of Hugh Nichols. "You're an old man—very nearly. This is the work for young men like me. Fellows, we're going to smash that door flat. Get ready. Give it your shoulders as you hit it, the pad of your shoulder muscles! It'll have to go down. Are you ready?"

"Ready!"

At that the gun spoke from the hand of El Cantor. It was answered by a shout as the human avalanche outside struck the door mightily. But the whir of the bullet had broken the ranks of the living battering ram, so it seemed, and the shock lacked solidity. So that although the door groaned, and there was the sharp creak of a half-broken hinge, it did not quite give way.

"No one hurt—he's shooting wild. Remember, boys, he has no light to see by. Try that door again, and when it goes down, remember—no guns! There's a woman in that room. We'll take El Cantor with our bare hands and then we'll break his neck for him!"

A hand found the arm of El Cantor.

"John," she said, "call out to them that you surrender. They'll murder you otherwise. They mean it—Hugh Nichols is a terrible fighting man. Surrender, John!" She raised her voice: "Hugh! Hugh! He has surrendered!"

"Let me hear him say it!" cried Nichols.

"You'll hear me," responded El Cantor calmly. "But you'll hear nothing else. Touch that door again, and you're a dead man, Nichols."

"Do you give me that dare?" cried Nichols outside the door. "Man, if there were ten like you I'd never take it—are you ready, friend?"

But El Cantor was at the door first, and a twist of the key freed the bolt of the lock. Then he stepped back.

"Hugh!" cried Margaret Swain. "He's one man against all of you!"

"Let him mind himself!" answered Nichols. "All together!"

They struck the door and, braced as they were for a heavy shock, when it flew open before them without the slightest rub of resistance, four men shot through the doorway and sprawled heavily upon the floor. And two more, just behind them, who had started to follow the rush, checked themselves too late and floundered into the kicking mass of feet and legs.

In another moment they, too, were down, and before the mass of humanity could untangle itself, El Cantor had leaped across the threshold. There arose before him only one man, and that was the sheriff himself, but it was the sheriff without a gun in his hand. True to the directions which he had given the rest of the men, he was making ready to enter that room with bare hands.

But bare hands against El Cantor were like empty air against the lightning flash. A wrist of whipcord, a fist of iron flashed into the face of big Walter Long, and he dropped back against the wall with a resounding thump, while through the hallway past him darted El Cantor.

The first man to regain his feet from the floor of the room was Hugh Nichols, raging, raving with fury. From the corner of his eye he saw the fugitive leap away around a corner of the hallway. But that was his only glimpse of El Cantor, who the next moment dived through an open window, landed rolling on the lawn outside, and was away.

20

Hen Pearson saw the fugitive in the very act of landing on the lawn. Mr. Pearson had brought along an old relic of his stage-driving days. Those had been times when the driver had to be a combination of horse tamer and adventurous knight. Mr. Pearson had qualified.

He had a wrist of iron, the vocabulary of a muleteer, and in the way of weapons he was fondest of an old double-barreled shotgun, which had been sawed off and which threw two handfuls of deadly slugs.

He recognized the man who was attempting to escape the instant he appeared at the window. Therefore, Mr. Pearson was ready, and when El Cantor struck the lawn, Mr. Pearson at one tremendous volley poured into his body two dozen or so chucks of lead.

In spite of this, El Cantor rolled lightly to his feet and sprang along to the hedge, over which he leaped, but not undisturbed. Ham Lawrence, the crack hunter and marvelous rifleman, whether at game on foot or at a standing target at any distance, was near at hand with his Winchester tucked under his arm.

He had seen El Cantor pass through the shower of lead from Hen Pearson's gun. He himself was determined that it should not be said that any creature could pass within twenty paces of his rifle muzzle and pass on alive, if he willed otherwise!

He tucked the butt of his favorite gun into the hollow of his shoulder, took a deliberate aim with a hand of iron, an arm like a rock supporting the long and glimmering barrel of his gun. Then as El Cantor reached the hedge he fired. He shot for the head, so confident was he even in the starlight.

When El Cantor bounded into the air, Ham was certain that it was the death leap. But when El Cantor landed on the farther side of the hedge, still running, he snapped up his rifle once more and through a gap in the hedge let drive again, once, twice, thrice and again. But El Cantor did not fall!

He sped on, and as he ran, a shrill, high-pitched whistle streamed back behind him on the wind. It was three times repeated in short blasts, and then three times again. Somewhere in the distance a horse neighed.

In the meantime two score of madmen were raging through the house of the parson and streaming outdoors again. The sheriff, gasping orders from one side of his battered mouth, ran for his horse and mounted it. Hugh Nichols did not have a mount at hand, of course, but he paid no attention to property rights. There were a dozen horses across the street, each with a saddle on its back. He picked the most likely and leaped onto its back.

"Hey, thief!" yelled the true owner, sprinting up.

"Out of my way!" shouted Nichols, and rushed past as if on wings.

The sheriff was before him leading the way, and the others rushed close at his heels.

A voice sang out: "Bullets don't faze him. It'll take knife work to settle his hash!"

Knife work? It would have taken a lightning flash to overtake him. Hugh Nichols had ridden thoroughbreds in many a hunting field and, therefore, he was no poor judge of speed. That horse beneath him had ample speed to account for itself in any other than racing company, but although Nichols overhauled the sheriff, they had not a chance.

The sharp whistle of the fugitive came again. Then out of the dark to one side flashed another horse, saddled, but without a rider. It shot past El Cantor—not past him, indeed, for as it flew along, it checked its stride ever so slightly and behold he was up on the back of the red bay stallion that shone like blood as it shot through the flare of light that rolled out through an open front doorway. Then away he went. As a bird flies out from the tree, so went Monsieur le Duc away from his pursuers.

They lost sight of him around the shoulder of the first hill beyond the town. When they reached that point, he was nowhere to be seen, and they pushed ahead, cursing and raging through the crowded hilltops.

But El Cantor had turned and was riding fast back to the town. He cast a half circle around it and found it alive with noise and confusion. Everyone was up. Everyone was dressed or half dressed. Swinging lanterns shone here and there. The windows were lighted. And now and then hoofbeats rattled away down the street as some other recruit for the posse, having caught, saddled and mounted his favorite horse, fled away through the night, hoping against hope that he might come up with the others in time to see the finale of that wild night's work.

El Cantor left Monsieur in a cluster of trees and remained there a moment with him, rubbing the velvet muzzle of the stallion with the palm of his hand, and laughing softly at the hubbub they had raised.

After a moment he went on toward the town, twisted between two outlying houses, and so came straight behind the home of Señor Alvarez. The garden was full of people. He lay flat on the cool ground near the gate and listened. What a torrent of chatter!

"It was all because he would marry Margaret Swain."

"But he didn't."

"It was a trick, then."

166

"Think of risking one's neck for the sake of such a thing."

"Perhaps it was all to have the pleasure of refusing her!"

Thus ran those soft voices in Spanish. El Cantor listened and smiled solemnly to himself. And when the rattling died down a little, he glided through the gate and waited in the shadow until there was a chance to see the girl alone. The other women had heard some vague tale from the street and were hurrying to learn the truth about it. Then Alvarez himself hurried into the house. And El Cantor, like a gliding wolf, was through the maze of bushes.

He came straight up before her and bowed.

"Señorita," said he, "I could not leave before I had seen you again!"

"Ah, heaven help me, it is he!" cried the girl. She ran to him and caught him by the shoulders. She shook him, or tried to shake him.

"Tell me! Tell me! You did *not* marry her!"

"I did not," said he.

"Mercy of heaven, what have I done?"

"Nothing. It is nothing."

"Ah, my dear! Can you forgive?"

"Such a little thing?"

"They might have murdered you!"

"Murder? It is my profession to have my neck in danger. It is nothing. But what did they do with you?"

"They told me about Señorita Swain. I could not stand it, dear; and I made Mateo tell them everything."

"It is he, then?" said El Cantor.

He removed her hands and held her away from him with a sudden sternness.

"It is Mateo who gave them what they wished to know?"

"Yes—no! Oh, what do you intend to do? You have not forgiven me—you have not forgiven me!"

"My dear," he announced, and his teeth gleamed behind a mirthless smile, "I always forgive a lady, no matter what she may have done. But Mateo—"

"Señor, it was not his fault. I told him that you had deceived me and made me a tool—"

"And, therefore, he was willing to betray me? Adios, señorita!"

"Señor, if I give the alarm—"

"Listen, foolish child," said El Cantor, "I cannot touch a girl, but consider your fat father and his family. Consider that, Alicia, and beware. I see you for the last time, but perhaps your friends will see me again!"

He was gone through the gate swiftly across the gap to his horse and then away down the outleading road until he came, some three miles out, to a great widespread ranch house in the Spanish style. He passed straight into the patio and cried out aloud: "Don Mateo! Don Mateo!"

A window was slammed open above him: "What is it, at this hour when honest men are sleeping?"

"Important news for Don Mateo."

"From whom?"

"The Señorita Alvarez."

"Ah?"

The obscure head disappeared. There was a stir in the house, and presently the door of the house was cast open and into the patio ran Don Mateo, half dressed, all breathless.

"From the Señorita Alicia!" he cried. "What is the—"

Then he saw El Cantor and understood. Instinctively his hand went where the revolver should have been, but there was no weapon on him.

"You have caught me!" he said calmly to the other, and folded his arms, disdaining either to flee or to beg for his life.

"What shall I do with you?"

"You consult me on that point? You are pleasant, señor."

"Don Mateo, you have betrayed me."

Don Mateo shrugged his shoulders.

"As you please," he remarked. "Some might say that I brought justice up with you; you call it betrayal."

"You confess then?"

"Confess?" exclaimed the young Mexican proudly. "I tell you, señor, that there has been nothing shameworthy in my conduct."

"At least," said El Cantor through his teeth, in a sudden fury, "at least, nothing that cannot be wiped away."

"I understand you perfectly. You mean in blood. Very well, señor, I am defenseless, but I shall not either run or kneel."

"Idiot," snarled El Cantor. "Do you dream that I mean murder? This is for you!"

He tossed a revolver through the air and Don Mateo caught it dexterously enough.

"Are you ready, Don Mateo? Then begin."

"I scorn an advantage, señor. You may move first."

"As you will!"

With that, he whipped out his revolver with a vicious speed. Long, long before the weapon in the hand of Don Mateo was leveled, Jingle Bells had pulled the trigger.

But there was only a loud click as the hammer descended—the faulty shell did not explode.

A fresh chamber was under the hammer, but El Cantor did not fire. For yonder was Don Mateo, his gun hanging at his side again.

"You did not fire, señor?" breathed El Cantor.

"I was so much slower," admitted Don Mateo, "that I had time to see your difficulty."

"And seeing that difficulty you did not take advantage?"

"My friend, I am not a murderer!"

169

"By heaven, Don Mateo, you have placed me under an obligation."

The youth could not restrain a smile.

"It was not a great gift. I would not have been able to hit you even if I had fired. I have no talent for this sort of thing."

El Cantor slowly shoved his revolver into the holster again.

"Señor," said he, "with your permission, I apologize for having called you from your sleep."

"Señor," said the other with an equal formality, "it has been a delight to see you again."

"You are kind."

"Indeed, señor, I feel that I have killed a most terrible enemy!"

El Cantor started. Then he thrust forth his hand.

"Don Mateo," said he, "it is true. I came here to destroy you. I leave you convinced that you have done nothing which a man of honor would not have done."

Their hands joined.

"And yet, my friend," said Don Mateo, "how did you manage to escape? But you were warned. You did not go to the town to-night."

"I was through the fire. I wear a charmed life," El Cantor replied. "And another thing: You may tell the charming Alicia that I have forgiven her, also."

"Before you go, Señor El Cantor, a glass of brandy—"

"I have no time. Adios."

"Adios, amigo."

And the fugitive, retiring to Monsieur le Duc, mounted and galloped away through the dark—the deepest dark of all, for the first early penciling of dawn was about to streak around the outlines of the hills.

21

Sheriff Walter Long, like many men of natural great good humor, was slow to anger but, once aroused, clung to his purpose like a bulldog. He clung to it now, while the others wearied of the chase and left its futility. Still he pushed straightway through the hills, working his men back and forth and combing every hollow until they were far from Gloryville and the light of the dawn began to stream up through the eastern sky.

But when they saw a living figure before them, it was not a mounted man, but a giant striding on foot across the brow of a hill against the sunrise. The sheriff recognized the outlines of that form, even at such a distance.

"We missed El Cantor," he said, "but we have the next best bet. It's Little Samuel!"

They swarmed around the huge man, reining in their horses with triumphant whoops.

Little Samuel affected to greet them with great joviality, taking off his hat and waving it.

"Well, Mister Sheriff," said he, "doggone me if it ain't been a lonesome walk across these here hills. There ain't nothin' more sort of convenient to me than havin' you along to keep me company—"

"Sam," broke in the sheriff, "where's your master?"

"Mister Sheriff," Little Samuel replied, "I ain't got no master. I'm a free man, Mr. Long."

"Mind your tongue," the sheriff declared, "or you'll be free no longer. Sam, I want to know where Jingle Bells may be found."

"I'm aimin' to find out the same thing," said Little Samuel. "I was figgerin' that one of you gents might know where I'd find him."

The sheriff could not help smiling, a grim smile in the faint morning light.

"Well, Sam," said he, "I suppose it'll have to be an argument. If—"

But here Hugh Nichols, riding up beside the sheriff, came fully before Little Samuel.

"You black rascal," Nichols remarked, but without passion in his voice, "do you think I have cause enough for putting you in jail?"

"Lord save us!" cried Little Samuel. "Mr. Nichols, you ain't gonna hold a little joke agin' me?"

"A little bullet," said Nichols, "which combed through the air a few feet above my head—was that a joke, Sam?"

"A joke?" Little Samuel exclaimed. "I'll tell a man. Why, sir, if I'd been aimin' to drill you clean, it wouldn't have been—"

"You can tell that to the judge," said the sheriff. "Sam, you're under arrest."

Little Samuel shouted with rage and apparently with wonder.

"It's a outrage," he declared. "They ain't nothin' agin' me. I ain't done nothin'. I'm—"

"Steady," said the sheriff solemnly, "because everything you say now may be used against you!"

The great mouth of Little Samuel closed tight; thereafter, he said not a word as he was escorted back toward the town. Only, when they had gone a quarter of a mile, the sheriff rode in front of his prisoner.

"Sam," he began, "I reckon you know that this is gonna be pretty bad trouble for you?"

"I ain't talkin'," said Little Samuel.

"Sure you ain't, except to me. I'm your friend, Sam. I ain't here to take no advantage of you in nothin'. I

172

want to see you and every other gent get a free break and a chance to clear themselves.

"But the skunk that I'm after is this here Jingle Bells. He's showed up the town and made a fool out of me, squeezing through the whole lot of us and gettin' clean away. We've got to have him and we're gonna get him.

"But if you could help us to land him pronto, it'd be a lot easier for you, Sam. I'll tell you this—if you was to give us a quick chance at him, you'd go plumb free and get a ticket to another town. You hear?"

Sam swallowed hard.

"But if you don't," said the sheriff, "you're in bad trouble."

"A little joke on Mr. Nichols—" began Sam lamely.

"A little joke? Lemme tell you, Sam, that that sort of a joke—you know what it is? It's kidnapin', and that's just the same as murder. Doggone if they couldn't hang you for a thing like that; or the least sort of a sentence they could give you would be fifteen years—"

"Hangin'—fifteen years—my Lord!" cried Little Samuel. "It ain't true!"

"You fool!" said the sheriff. "Don't you see that this scoundrel El Cantor has made a tool out of you, and that he has given you the slip to let you stand the punishment while he gets away if he can?"

Little Samuel considered, and then he shook his head.

"If I was to talk about El Cantor, d'you know what he'd do to me?"

"What could he do?"

"Burnin' alive would be about his size," decided Little Samuel thoughtfully.

"So tell us what we want to know, and we'll clap him behind bars—that's the end of him!"

"Him? Bars ain't made that'll keep him safe!" Little Samuel announced. "He'd squeeze out through a knot-hole, dog-gone him!"

173

No persuasion could move him. And so, formally arrested for the crime of making an assault upon Hugh Nichols and illegally confining his person, the big man was herded back toward Gloryville.

It was full morning, with a hot sun riding high, when they arrived. But Gloryville was quiet as night. For the strain of all that had happened since midnight had made men and women sleep late. As for Hugh Nichols, he found a room in the hotel, flung himself upon it, and slept as one drugged with fatigue until midafternoon. Then he rose, drank two steaming cups of thick, black coffee, and then went to find Margaret Swain.

She and her father had been accommodated at the parsonage. The parson himself was met by Nichols in the garden of the old house—a pale and shaken parson walking nervously back and forth. When the gate slammed behind Nichols, he jumped as if he had heard a gun explode. The Easterner introduced himself and was greeted with a faint handclasp.

"Mr. Nichols," he said, "the world has gone mad, or I have gone mad! Or perhaps you have a theory. How did El Cantor break into the house without being seen last night?"

"It is a hard problem," admitted Nichols, "unless he was in here all the time."

"Before they came?"

"Yes."

"No, no!" the parson asserted. "I know that he is a man with nerves of steel, but not even he would have dared to do such a thing. He could not! And yet, Nichols," he added, clutching the arm of the Easterner, "when I was in that room with him, when the rest of you were at the doors trying to beat them in, his voice was as cool as yours or mine at this moment! At this moment!"

In the house, Nichols found Margaret Swain at once;

174

the parson brought him to her in the library, and she stood up, pale and smiling, to greet him. All the weariness dropped from the body of Nichols; he stood before her like a thoroughbred trembling at the post and ready for the race, so eager were his eyes, so tense was his smile.

"Dear Hugh," she said, "I'm as grateful to you as though everything had worked out as you planned."

"Only tell me one thing," he said, still holding her hands. "How has your father managed? I didn't have a chance to talk to him about it last night."

"He is saved."

"Peggy, I have guessed at a devilish strange thing. It is this El Cantor."

"Yes."

"You sold yourself to him?"

"Hugh, he wouldn't have me, at the last minute."

"Why, Peggy, no wonder. We were outside the doors making it too hot for him!"

"No, no!"

She raised her hand to stop him.

"But what else?" he asked.

"Nothing could have stopped him if he had wanted to do it. I know nothing could have stopped him!"

The smile of Hugh Nichols was wan.

"You'll make him out another Napoleon," he said.

"Do you know," said the girl slowly, "that I almost feel that way about him—as though there were a fate working in him."

"Nonsense, Peggy! You've had too much excitement lately. There is no fate in that cunning rascal."

"Can you explain, then, why the rascal has thrown away sixty-five thousand dollars?"

"Ah? Unsecured?"

"Not a penny of security, except the honor of my father."

175

"An ample bond even for a thief," said Hugh NIchols.

"Not among bankers, when we wanted help. No, Hugh, there is something strange about him, something more than meets the eye."

"You are afraid of him?"

"Fear? Well, I suppose that I am."

They sat beside the window, he feeling that he had been pushed away from her by their few moments of conversation.

"And what will he do now?" asked Nichols.

"I have less idea than you have."

"I have a very clear one. He will use the first opportunity to hound you into a marriage, claiming your promise."

"He surrendered that claim."

"When he was afraid that the rope would be around his neck the next moment."

"Hugh, you are unjust to him."

"My dear Peggy, you are interested in that rascal. On my honor, you are!"

"I?"

Her laughter grew weak and then broke sharply off. She found herself staring at Nichols.

"Do you think so?" she asked. "I don't know, really."

Poor Nichols gaped.

"Good gad, Peggy," said he, "you are not meaning that I guessed right?"

"I don't know what I'm meaning, except that my head swims. I can't understand him, Hugh."

"But, Peggy, to think seriously of such a fellow of— of wild reputation! By heavens, Peggy, you don't mean that you are seriously fond of him?"

"I never put that question to myself until this moment, Hugh."

"But the answer has to be only one thing—that of course such a supposition is perfectly absurd. Say that,

Peggy. Otherwise, I'll lose my mind. Because—"

She could see by the brightness of his eyes what was coming, he was so picked up and carried away by his own emotion. She tried to stop him by raising her hand. But he shook his head as though to brush aside her protest.

"Because I've come down here with a heart on fire with very high hopes, Peggy. I've come down here trusting that you would not have called on me for help unless you thought kindly of me, trusting, Peggy, that I might dare to tell you something which has been in me for a long time—that I love you, Peggy!"

She had twisted her hands together and watched him with a look of regretful wistfulness.

"I'm so sorry that it came out, Hugh," said she.

"Is it such a hopeless case?"

"I can say a thousand fine things of you. But not the one thing you want to hear."

"Peggy, will you tell me one thing?"

"Anything I can that you can ask, of course."

"Before that wild affair of last night—Well, to put it another way: At this time yesterday, would you have been more open to persuasion than you are now?"

"I hardly know what you mean."

"If I had asked you to marry me yesterday at this time—"

"I would have told you that I was under a bond to another man."

"And if that bond had not existed?"

She fell into thought.

"I don't know. I think perhaps I should have."

He stood up.

"Then it was what happened last night that changed you. This fellow El Cantor—Jingle Bells, whatever his name may be—"

She flushed at this.

"His name is John Albert."

"Are you sure of that?"

She grew still more red, but could not make any other answer. For, in her heart of hearts, she knew that she was not sure.

"At any rate," said Hugh Nichols, "we'll find a way to remove him from the scene. Peggy, you're not the type that becomes infatuated easily. And that's why I tremble!"

She cried at him. "You really talk as though I'd throw myself at him! Hugh, how can you speak of me in such a way?"

"I'm sorry," he said gloomily. "But I begin to see what a devilish thing the whole tangle is! And it makes me heartsick!"

There was no rest that day for the sheriff. While Gloryville was in a swirl with the happenings which had focused on the parsonage, there was other trouble in the air, trouble of a far more dreadful significance. And that was the slaying of old Martin Hendon, a good man and a well-known citizen who had retired from ranching only the year before and was a resident of Gloryville— almost its richest man.

There was no harm in Mart Hendon. There was no pride in his money, no vainglory. He was simply a gentle, companionable old fellow of nearly seventy, as unpretending as a child. And this was the man who was found dead in his house.

He had gone out to find the cause of the riot at the parsonage, it appeared, and while he was gone the thieves had broken in. They obtained little for their trouble except a few articles of silver. In the midst of their work, old Hendon returned and fairly blundered upon them.

He was not armed. That made the hideousness of the crime all the more appalling. Indeed, he had not carried a gun for many years, but the thieves had knocked him

178

down, tied him hand and foot, and finally—perhaps maddened by the influence of some whisky which was among their loot—they had brained him with an ax. Such was the tale that took the worthy sheriff out on the road for five hours of fierce riding as he combed the countryside.

For the two murderers were known. One was a tall, long-striding fellow, according to the footprints; the other was short, and had remarkably small feet. And Mrs. Hendon could testify that a tall man and a short one, traveling together, had called at Hendon's house to try to persuade him to give them jobs on his ranch. He had refused, merely because he was in no need of cowpunchers. But they had left in a fury.

The sheriff came back fairly exhausted and unsuccessful. And the next thing on his program was not rest, but an interview with big Sam. He took the prisoner into his office, with irons on his hands and feet.

"Now, Sam," said he, "I'm gonna make a bargain with you, and you're gonna take it. You're gonna give me enough information to put El Cantor in jail for life, and I'm gonna see that you go free."

"Could you do that?" asked Little Samuel, sighing as he thought of the iron bars which walled his cell around, and the hard little cot.

"I could do that. I could fix things up with the district attorney plumb easy. Him and me are after the big crooks, not the little ones."

"I got to wait and take my chance," said Little Samuel lugubriously. And there he stuck.

The fear of the prison bars was not half so great as his dread of El Cantor's vengeance in case of betrayal.

22

There were five men by the fire in the "jungle"; there was one man in the highest tip of the great tree which rose above this haven of the tramps. He kept good lookout in the moonlight for the approach of any strangers of a formidable respectability in their appearance. For these were stirring and unhappy times with the hobos.

The good men of Gloryville, enraged by the murder of poor old Mart Hendon at the hands of vagabonds, were quartering the countryside; and when they found a loafer they thought nothing of riding him on a rail and then rolling him in a coating of tar and strewing him with feathers.

People who do not know think that shame is the only punishment in this; but others, more wise, understand what trouble it needs to remove the tar from even one spot on a finger. So, the word of the reign of terror having gone forth, this small company was gathered here. It had been herded in from varying directions.

They met here for a brief rest, the cooking of an immense pot of slumgullion, and after a sleep of two or three hours they would be off again, each hunting the horizon, each in dread of those terrible riders from Gloryville.

The stew had been eaten, the tramps were reposing right and left, when the lookout gave a warning cry. By the time he reached the ground the others had rolled up their belongings, or pocketed them, and were ready to go. The lookout announced only one rider approaching. And at this there was a general groan of disgust. What was one man to be feared?

"He might have a whole slough of others behind him," suggested the lookout.

"And again, he might not. We'll lay for this bloke. Jerry—here, you sit here by the fire. The rest of us'll sneak back in the bushes and wait. When he comes up, give him your lip, old kid. And if he gets rough we'll swarm all over him."

"That's pretty hard on the rest of you, ain't it?" suggested the unwilling Jerry. "Here's Steve Grenda. He ain't so big that he's gonna get into trouble with most folks. He's got a better chance, too, of gettin' away. Steve, will you take the job?"

Steve, it appeared, was not altogether unwilling. He sat down by the fire, hugging his knees and smoking a pipe—a little man with a ragged-rimmed derby on his head and a pair of undersized shoes upon his extremely small feet. In the meantime his companions vanished, and they were hardly out of sight before the stranger appeared, riding right through the brush and coming into the flickering circle of the firelight.

"Well, partner?" he hailed.

Steve shrugged his shoulders and grunted; he offered no further greeting. So the stranger looked calmly around him and allowed his horse to wander closer to the fire. It stretched out its head toward the flames like a curious child. It was a magnificent red bay with a skin that glistened as if oiled in the firelight.

"You are having a peaceful time," said El Cantor with perfect calmness. "Why have your friends left you?"

"Friends?" echoed Steve Grenda.

The rider swept his hand toward the ground. In fact, the depressions which many footfalls had left were all the more visible because the slant firelight, striking across them, filled them with shadow.

"Well?" grunted Steve, making no concessions even to this evidence.

"The size of your feet, man," said El Cantor with a contemptuous impatience—"the size of your feet! They would not fit in one tenth of those clodhopper trails."

"Who may you be to ask?" rumbled Steve, bristling like the bull terrier that he was.

"A man with his eyes in his head," returned El Cantor. "Besides, your feet are extraordinarily small—"

This thought, as he voiced it aloud, seemed to strike him so forcibly that he started in the saddle and looked fixedly down to the little man by the fire. The latter glowered savagely back to him.

"Why," said he, "leave my feet be!"

The rider merely smiled again.

"You are a foolish fellow," he declared, "to rattle along like that. You do yourself a great deal of harm."

"With saps like you," said Steve furiously, "I dunno that I give a hoot how I stand."

"You don't," observed the other, "and that's the pity of it. Because we're the only ones who can help you."

"Help me?"

"Yes."

"Help me from what?"

"Hanging," said El Cantor.

The eyes of the little man by the fire glinted back and forth, as a dog's eyes flash when it glimpses two approaching. And his stubby fist slipped back to his hip pocket.

"Now, you slick-faced dick, you," he whined in a muted fury, "what are you after?"

"You talk like a jackass, man," said El Cantor. "If I were a detective, would I come up to you like this when you are surrounded by your friends, the gunmen, in the bushes yonder?"

Steve Grenda stood up.

"I dunno," he declared thoughtfully. "I dunno about

182

this line of talk. You got a fast-workin' tongue. But I dunno about trusting you too far. It ain't good sense."

"Very well," El Cantor remarked. "But what do you think has brought me here?"

"Nothin' but accident, bo!"

El Cantor smiled. "A lucky accident," said he.

"Lucky for what?"

"For me, you fool!"

With that he dropped the reins across the neck of the red bay, and while a tap of his heel sent Monsieur le Duc flying away at a round gallop, El Cantor leaned sidewise from the saddle like a swooping hawk.

His lean, powerful arms gripped about Steve Grenda, and that worthy was snatched up before the rider in a trice.

As for the watchers, they had time to utter one yell of astonishment. But when they raised their guns to fire they hesitated. There was more chance of killing Steve with their bullets than there was of dropping the rider. Before they could make up their minds, El Cantor and the horse and the captive were across the thicket into the open country beyond.

Steve Grenda made a brief fight and a bitter one until a hand of steel caught a wrist and doubled his arm behind his back. Then, with the bone threatening to snap at every instant, he was helpless.

"What are you drivin' at?" he snarled.

But the captor made no reply. His cruel, contemptuous face did not alter; not a spoken syllable was returned to Steve. But presently he was secured with both hands bound behind his back, and in this fashion he was forced to run forward in front of the horseman—run until his breath was failing him.

So they came over the hill into full view of Gloryville by night. At that sight Grenda stopped with a shout of despair. He turned to fling himself at the other, even with his bound hands. But he was struck down into senselessness, and when he wakened again he lay bound hand and foot and gagged in a shrouding darkness among shrubs; but where he was he could not tell, for he was unable to move. And the gag which closed his throat was nearly strangling him.

But that place in which he lay was none other than the backyard of the house of Sheriff Walter Long; and in the harness shed the weary sheriff, too harassed with worries to sleep, was busily patching a broken girth. He looked up from that work with his needle poised and observed before him none other than the much-wanted Jingle Bells, with a long revolver hanging from his hand.

The gun was not leveled upon the sheriff, as though the mere show of it should be enough to a sensible man. The sheriff appreciated keenly this tribute to his intelligence, but he glowered blackly upon the other.

"Jingle Bells," said he, "damn me if you ain't up to more deviltry! What is it now?"

"I am about to perform an act of charity."

"Of which?"

"Charity."

"To what, might I ask?"

"To you, sheriff."

"I got to be patient," said the sheriff, "while you got the drop on me. But what might you mean?"

"I am about to make a trade with you. For the sake of the freedom of Little Samuel, I'll turn over to you a bona-fide murderer, a real rare one, sheriff."

"You're talkin' crazy," said the sheriff. "What murderer?"

"What's the one you most want just now?"

"Not one—I want the bloody pair that slaughtered good old Mart Hendon. I want them bad, too!"

"Very well, sheriff, I have one of the men!"

"What?"

184

"Look at this!"

He tossed a half dozen silver spoons down before the sheriff.

"This stuff was in his pocket. There's an 'H' on them, as you see."

"As I see! God bless me, ain't I ate with 'em many and many a time? Oh, Jingle Bells, bring me to the gent that you got these here from, and you can have ten prisoners in exchange!

"But," he added, pausing, "how'll we make the exchange? Am I gonna go to the jail and bring out Little Samuel, while you stay back here with your man? No, no, Jingle Bells, that's too slim. I'd never see any of the three of you again."

"You may take your time, sheriff, and do it in your own way. I'll wait here until you have taken the murderer in."

"You'll wait here, Jingle Bells, and take a chance on me sneakin' back with a couple of hands to help me—"

"My dear sheriff," smiled El Cantor, "you are absurd. Of course I know you are a man of honor!"

23

They sat on opposite sides of the library table at the Swain house like two generals laying forth a plan of campaign. And if Henry Swain were serious, Hugh Nichols was despairing.

"You've overrated what she's told you," declared the father. "You've far overrated the importance of what she has said, Hugh. Because she's extremely outspoken, and is sure to say a little bit more than is in her mind."

"Mr. Swain," said the younger man, "I have tried to think that. But it's something more than what she's said. When she speaks of this fellow John Albert, as he calls himself, there's a change in her voice and a change in her eye. Those things have a meaning. She may be outspoken, but she has never been emotional."

Swain pondered for a moment. "Then tell me," he inquired, "how far you think that the thing might go."

"I think I know," big Hugh Nichols replied. "It will go to a marriage. Particularly if she's opposed by us. One can't say a word against this El Cantor. She fires up at once and begins to defend him. I've noticed that."

"Marriage!" breathed Swain. "Marriage to an infernal adventurer, a nameless rascal, an outlawed thief and ruffian, a gunfighter, a notorious scoundrel like that? I tell you, Hugh, I'd far rather that the ranch had been lost and that my ruin had taken us both out of this section of the country."

"What does the section matter to him?" asked Nichols despondently. "I've thought of that. I've thought of persuading her to leave this district for a time. But I tell you, Mr. Swain, the fellow would follow us. He would be away after you like a bloodhound."

"Do you think so?"

"I know so, Mr. Swain. There's that much devil in him. The higher you build the wall the surer he is to climb it!"

"But the law is on him, NIchols. His departure from the country can be barred."

"Can it, though?"

"Certainly!"

"But what can be held against him? What that is serious, I mean?"

"What? Why, man, the whole world knows that he's an outlawed—"

"But for what?"

"Why, for kidnaping you, for one thing."

"He did me no harm. And, after all, I'd be ashamed to appear in such a case. It would make me a laughingstock at home."

"But there are other things. He shot down two of my men—"

"In a fair fight. I think you'd find it hard to get a conviction from a Western jury on such a matter. They won't jail one man for beating two others in a fair fight, particularly where neither wound was mortal!"

"But the scene at the parson's house—"

"After all, Mr. Swain, what did that really amount to? Your daughter had agreed—"

"Had been bribed—bought, Hugh."

"Would the law feel that? She had agreed to marry him. When he came to marry her, according to the agreement, he was set upon by armed men. That wouldn't look particularly honorable for our side of the case!"

"In the name of heaven, do you mean to say that if he stands his trial—"

"Just now, while feeling is high about the affair, he might have trouble. But in a few months, there won't be a shadow to raise against him. Already people are beginning to speak favorably of him because he caught one of the two devils who murdered old Mr. Hendon. This fellow Grenda has confessed, and now they're apt to get the second man."

"I've heard that. And it convinces me that there's only one way out of the mess, and that's to take my girl away from this place and keep her away until the ridiculous romance is well out of her head!"

"Very well, sir. It sounds like the only hope. But I warn you that El Cantor will make a desperate effort to follow you."

"The law will help you keep him back. With that handicap I may win. And the first real change of scene may bring my girl to her senses. It is a sort of hypnotism, at the best!"

He tried to persuade Hugh Nichols to go with them, but the young man refused.

"I've given up all my own hope," he told the rancher.

"I've never seen her so friendly to you," urged Swain. "She always refers to you as 'dear Hugh.' Bless me, man, what better could you have?"

"I'd rather have her hate me. Hate is nearer to love than friendship is—a very great deal. And she's too friendly with me now. Love implies a little touch of mystery. And there's no mystery about me. Peggy has discovered it and there you are! It will never come out well for me. Never. She has come to know me too well. You never hear of well-acquainted people actually falling in love."

There he stuck, and the very next day said his farewell and started back to New York. He did not go far in advance of the others, however. That same day, Mr. Swain informed his daughter that he had received intelligence from his sister who lived in south Italy telling him that her affairs were in a serious crisis and that he must go to her at once.

And Margaret Swain, listening to this grave story, waited for a moment, watching her father with quietly amused eyes, plainly telling him in her silence that she well understood what was in his mind.

But she consented. She asked for three days. He gave her one. And, for twenty-four hours, he saw her anxiety increasing. He well knew what it meant. She was waiting for the coming of El Cantor.

Yet that time wore away—a time of suspense to the rancher. Then they stepped into the buckboard which carried them to Cranton, and all the way across the dusty road her eyes were strained toward the horizon, as if she expected El Cantor to come out upon them with a rush at any moment.

Still he did not come. Cranton loomed in sight. They stood upon the station platform at last. The train rumbled in. And now they were climbing up the steps—now they were in their seats. Still the girl held tense with suffering eyes, but when the engine lurched ahead and then the long rumble of the starting train began, her nerves snapped, and she broke into silent weeping.

It was a painful thing for Henry Swain to watch, but he felt that the first and the longest step to her salvation had been taken.

In four days they stood on the deck of a great liner which was rushing across the Atlantic. And every knot that stretched behind them was a comfort to Henry Swain. They passed between the Pillars of Hercules. They swept on south until at last they docked in the colorful, noisy port of Naples.

But though Margaret smiled and strove to put on a cheerful pretense, she could not deceive her father. She was pale, and she had passed out of her girlhood in the last fortnight. She was already on the verge of full womanhood.

Their baggage was to follow them on the train. They themselves were picked up by Aunt Elizabeth's carriage and taken southward through the rolling hills and over the white roads.

"Peggy," said her father suddenly, giving way to the impulse which had been making a lump in his throat for the last two weeks, "for heaven's sake, drop him from your mind. He is not worth a minute of your thought!"

He could feel her shudder under his touch, but there

189

was no other response. An hour later, they were in the house of Aunt Elizabeth. She had been informed as to what she could say about her "financial crisis," by a long letter detailing the facts as they stood in the Far West concerning El Cantor, and she was ready to play her part.

But first of all, she gave them tea under the pergola which stood on the edge of the cliff, with sharply terraced gardens dropping toward the blue sea. It was a tiny harbor with a rocky island at its mouth and fishers' little boats heeling over before the wind. At the bottom of the cliff was the town, a ragged strip of squalor and of color.

While Peggy Swain forgot herself long enough to smile at the beauty of the place and then ran down to investigate a strip of enormous hollyhocks, her aunt leaned to her brother.

"This is a very bad case," said she.

"How do you mean?" he asked. "How can you tell?"

"Love," the maiden aunt replied, "is like steam. If it is let off in talk—all very well. But when it isn't turned into words—my dear brother, it's as serious as a disease. How are we to cure the child?"

"Have you no handsome counts to produce, Elizabeth? Have you sat here with your hands folded ever since I wrote to you that we were coming?"

"I have plenty of them—if she will but look. But for my part, I'd rather have her married to an American outlaw. Well, well, dear brother, every man to his own taste!"

She would *not* look. So much was plain after three weeks of entertainments.

"Let her have some solitude," Aunt Elizabeth suggested then, and straightway took them out for a sail on her own little yacht.

190

She herself had the helm. There were two red-shirted fishermen glad to take a day's work for the liberal pay of the lady, and so they slid smoothly down the bay with the wind in the belly of the leg-of-mutton sail. They rounded the island at the mouth of the harbor by mid-morning.

The sea beyond was smooth as glass—certainly there could be no danger here! And yonder were the fishing craft making out, or already far away, hull down against the blue horizon, little winking bits of sail.

So Aunt Elizabeth, instead of putting straight into one of the coves of the island, put straight out for sea. At this, her brother grew anxious.

"This devilish wind is all very well for running out," said he. "But how about coming home again?"

"Why, my dear," his sister explained, "don't you think that we can go into the wind with this boat? Tush! It eats into it like a full-rigged ship—no, better, far better. I'll show you."

So saying, she made a starboard tack that ran her aslant through the mouth of the harbor. They left the foaming teeth of a rock ridge twenty feet away as they slid through the little harbor mouth.

"By heavens, Elizabeth," cried her brother. "Don't do that again! This is worse than a bucking horse on the edge of a cliff. I can't swim, you know!"

She merely smiled at him, and Margaret, from the bows where she was watching the trembling of the wind in the sail and listening to the rush of the water, laughed for the first time since they left home.

"Go on, then," said Henry Swain to his sister. "It seems to be putting some spirit in Peggy. You may sail to the devil and back if you can accomplish that! But have you pirates in these days and these waters?"

He pointed back to an odd craft with a wide shell of a hull that skimmed across the water blown along by a

191

great clumsy-looking rectangular sail. But despite its queer appearance, the craft was a notable sailer. It was gaining on Elizabeth Swain's little yacht at every moment.

"That looks like a boat out of an Egyptian tomb," said Elizabeth. "However, they get all manner of craft in these waters. They come across from the African coast —the same sort of craft that they have been using for centuries, you know. But why piratical, if you please?"

"Because the rascal is following us."

"Nonsense! He's simply making out to sea."

"Tack again, and we'll see."

"Very well, then."

She shouted to Peggy to crouch beneath the swing of the boom, then spun her helm, and came about and rocked away on the port tack. The wind freshened. The little craft began to dip her nose through the wave-tops and cast back stinging little volleys of spray.

"Look!" cried Swain. "By heavens, the rascal is coming straight after us!"

His sister stared aft with a frown. Yonder, in fact, came the queer stranger, overhauling them by leaps and bounds.

"He's playing tag with us, that's all," she decided in a peremptory tone which showed that she didn't like it. "The rascal sees that he has the foot of us and he's running around showing off. See him come!"

As the stranger filled on the port tack and gathered way, he began to eat up the space between them rapidly enough, to be sure.

"I don't like it!" confessed Swain.

"You're really silly, Henry," Aunt Elizabeth said in reproof. "Of course this harbor is as safe as my drawing-room floor! And as for pirates—why, you can see for yourself that there are only two men on that craft!"

Now that it was so near, they could make out, in fact,

that there was only the man at the helm who seemed a cunning steersman, and a single sailor of gigantic size to work the ropes.

"He must be a Hercules, that fellow," their hostess said, "or he could never handle that sail single-handed. Isn't he black, Henry? The sun is in my eyes, and I can't make him out very clearly."

"Black?" cried her brother. "Black? Good heavens, Elizabeth!"

"What's the matter now? Henry, you've actually turned hysterical!"

"Elizabeth, I've told you about Little Samuel."

At this she started. And as she looked back to her brother she gasped: "Do you really think—"

"Look at Peggy!"

She was standing up straight, her face lifted and her eyes ablaze with joy as she looked back to the stranger.

"She knows!" said Henry Swain. "You can see it in her face."

"How could he come?"

"Don't ask me how. Elizabeth, put about and run back for the harbor."

"Are you actually afraid?"

"I tell you, my dear, that you don't know that young demon. There is nothing past him! Here's Peggy coming aft to us to see them better. The devil is in it!"

The stranger had now advanced so close that it was easy to make out every line in her and the features of the two men who composed her crew, and there was no doubt remaining. Yonder was the huge bulk of Little Samuel, singing. And what was he singing? A song in praise of El Cantor!

At the helm was El Cantor himself, laughing now and waving his hat to them in a broad circle.

"Go about, Elizabeth!" cried Henry Swain.

She put her helm over without a word, and, as the

boom swung across, the yacht lost headway and hung poised, fighting to gain way once more. At the same time the pursuer luffed and only the original headway wafted the broad-bottomed boat along. Even so, she came swiftly on. Now Little Samuel was at the helm, and El Cantor stood at the rail.

"Mr. Swain," he cried, "will you permit me to call at sea, so to speak?"

"The devil fly away with him," said Elizabeth Swain. "He's a handsome youngster. No wonder he turned Peggy's head. What will you do, Henry?"

He put his answer to her into his answer to the outlaw. For, leaping up, he cried: "Young man, bear off from us. Do you hear? And if—"

El Cantor waved a hand as though to brush the other out of his mental horizon.

"Peggy," he called, "will you come aboard with us for a spin out to sea and back?"

"You impertinent young fool!" thundered Henry Swain, "if you dare—"

"Henry!" cried his sister. "Stop her!"

He turned in time to see his daughter standing poised on the outer edge of the yacht as the little boat filled away on her new course, heeling far over and so lifting the girl high above the level of the water. At the same time the odd ship of El Cantor glided in under the lee of their craft and there was El Cantor back at the wheel, handling it like a sensitive horse, while big Samuel stood with legs braced far apart.

"Jump, Peggy!" cried El Cantor.

"Peggy, are you mad?" shouted her father, leaping for her.

But she was already in the air. Her leap and an upward fling of the yacht had pitched her high, and now she rushed down straight into the arms of Little Samuel.

He received her as lightly as a feather, swung her

around, and there she crouched low on the deck with an arm flung up across her face, as if to cover it from the scorn and the rage of her father.

At the same time, the wide-bottomed boat of El Cantor, its sail filling with the wind again, leaped away across the water, and the yacht whipped off on the opposite tack.

"I'll come about after them!" cried Elizabeth.

"Hold your course," said her brother bitterly. "He has her at last. It would take a greater power than mine to take her from him again!"